Getting killed was part of my job, but neither Jen nor Clarice had signed on for that.

The gunfire kept Clarice's crying at a constant keen, making even Jen sob every once in a while. The men on the hill wanted to kill us, but they wanted to have some fun doing it.

I lifted Jen's Colt from her holster.

"I'm going to start returning fire," I told her. "You take the kid and start running for the timber as soon as I do."

Jen didn't argue. She probably would have stayed and done her own shooting, but it was the kid she was worried for.

My rifle was in the scabbard on my animal. All I had was my .44. But it would be enough to force our hunters to take cover while Jen and Clarice made it to the woods.

"Now!" I shouted.

I started firing like crazy, emptying Jen's gun into the air in the general direction of their position. This got the response that I'd hoped for.

Just as I got into a crouching position, preparing to throw myself onto the trail and roll into the relative safe haven of the forest—just then the air became furious with two men who had decided to give up playing and start firing in earnest. I had to get to my rifle—a repeater and ammunition were the only way we were going to survive.

Otherwise, they would start with me. And after I was dead, they'd have Jen to have some fun with. Maybe even the same kind of fun they'd had with Clarice's mother . . .

ED GORMAN

CAVALRY MAN
POWDER KEG

HarperTorch
An Imprint of HarperCollinsPublishers

This is a work of fiction. Names, characters, places, and incidents are products of the author's imagination or are used fictitiously and are not to be construed as real. Any resemblance to actual events, locales, organizations, or persons, living or dead, is entirely coincidental.

◆

HARPERTORCH
An Imprint of HarperCollins*Publishers*
10 East 53rd Street
New York, New York 10022-5299

First HarperTorch paperback printing: August 2006

HarperCollins®, HarperTorch™, and ◆ ™ are trademarks of
HarperCollins Publishers Inc.

Printed in the United States of America

Visit HarperTorch on the World Wide Web at www.harpercollins.com

10 9 8 7 6 5 4 3 2 1

TO DENNY BURGESS, LONG OVERDUE

Acknowledgments

My thanks to Linda and Kate Siebels,
for their invaluable help with this book

CAVALRY MAN
POWDER KEG

PART ONE

Chapter 1

Never bothered me much to pull a gun on a man, but a woman was a different matter. Even if it was 1883, despite a lot of new contraptions like electric lights and telephones, women still needed a whole lot of protection.

The place was Kansas City, the Elite Hotel, room 227, six minutes after midnight. I was sitting in my dark room listening to the giddy Friday night noise from the casino one floor below me and the whorehouse one floor above me.

I had been planning on visiting the latter but I'd had so much bad luck with the former that night that I wasn't much in the mood, not even for the kind of soft and perfumed young flesh a man could find in a good-sized city like that one.

I was trying to think about my job there so I wouldn't have to think about how much I'd lost at the casino. Faro had never been kind to me. But then neither had poker or blackjack. Gambling was one of my curses.

The knock came at nine minutes after midnight,

which I knew because the moon was cordial enough to shine on the railroad watch that sat ticking away on the arm of my chair.

Frantic. One knock followed almost instantly by another.

I'd been warned that a man named Fred Cartel was going to try and kill me that night and the way my luck was running, he might just have been able to pull it off.

"Please, please, Mr. Ford. Please open the door." It was a woman's voice.

Fred had a lot of imagination, which was how he'd managed to embezzle so much money from the veterans' hospital there. Because it was a federal institution and because I was a federal agent, I'd been sent there to arrest him, even though it wasn't my area. I specialized in weapons threats—new technology, better explosives, more modern delivery systems, things like that. I was in the area, though. I'd been working a job in Wichita so Washington had wired me to take a train and make the nab. Fred must have consulted a crystal ball because right after I'd checked in that afternoon, I received a large envelope containing $5,000 in fresh new American currency. The letter that went along with the money said that Mrs. Fred had a cousin who worked for our office in Wichita and he had tipped her that I was coming to arrest Fred. She said that Fred would come to see me that night and that I should treat him politely because he suffered from what some folks considered a pretty bad temper. And, in fact, had said that if I didn't take his money he might just kill me. I guess that qualified as a bad temper.

But Fred was clever.

He was going to trap me.

What better way to get me to open my door so he could shoot me than to have a woman pretend that she was in some kind of dire emergency? And when I opened the door—

Fred would show me just how bad his temper really was.

I decided to make the surprise on her.

"Just a minute," I said, sounding calm.

I was almost glad for this. A good shootout is a way to keep a man from thinking about his gambling losses.

The surprise was simple enough.

I crossed to the door on tiptoe and then yanked the door inward without warning, shoving my .44 in her face as I did so. I didn't give her time to scream. I yanked her inside with my hand and kicked the door shut with my heel.

Before I got the lamp turned up, I shoved her on the bed. Then I got the lamp going.

And then she said: "You're going to feel very stupid, Noah."

And she sure wasn't kidding about that.

"Oh, God, Susan, I didn't have any idea it was you."

"I figured as much—unless you'd changed a lot."

Tom Daly was one of my best friends in the agency. We'd worked a couple dozen assignments together since the war. And once he ran into a burning building on the suicide mission of hauling me out. He saved my life when not even the volunteer firemen would give it a try. Tom was a fine husband, father, friend. I would add worker to that except he had a bottle problem. He disappeared on benders, and bosses, for some reason, frown on that.

A year earlier, Tom had come under suspicion of stealing and selling the location of a secret government munitions laboratory. He still worked for the agency but he was angry that he'd even been suspected. And he had a fixed idea about who had stolen and sold the information. The boss tired of Tom's anger so he moved him to a different office.

I'd known they'd settled in Kansas City so I'd wired ahead to let them know that I was coming. But when I got to their house that day, nobody was home.

That night, after midnight, Tom's wife Susan, an appealingly slight, dark-haired woman, was lying across the bed where I'd just shoved her.

"I'm really sorry, Susan. I thought you were dodging for some embezzler who threatened to kill me."

She sat up, smiled.

"Same old dull life, huh?"

I laughed.

"Yeah. But why so late, and where's Tom? I stopped by but nobody was home."

She shook her head.

"He doesn't want to see you."

"Why not?"

"He thinks you'll talk him out of it. You know the kind of influence you have on him. He always jokes that when he grows up he wants to be just like you. Big, strong, handsome. But he's only half-joking."

I had to laugh.

"You don't think I'm any of those things, do you? And be honest. In fact, you never cared for me much."

"You're really putting me on the spot. Thanks."

"You never looked happy to see me. And the times I kept Tom out drinking—you ragged on me a lot more than you ragged on him."

She sighed. Looked down at her hands.

"You're a nice-looking man—but so's Tom. And you're clever and decent—and Tom's those things, too. His older brother died in the war. Tom was always so used to playing second fiddle—having somebody to look up to—that when he met you, you took the place of his brother Bob. So, no, I don't see you as this kind of dime-novel hero that you are to him. I just wish he had a little more confidence about himself." With no warning at all, her green eyes glistened with tears. "But now he's got too much confidence. And that's what he's afraid you'll talk him out of."

She paused. "But I have to say, for all the times you two went out drinking, you're the one who got him to stop. He wouldn't even listen to me when I talked to him about how much he drank. But he listened to you and I'll always be grateful to you for that."

I went over to the bureau and picked up my sack of Bull Durham and my cigarette papers. As I rolled my cigarette, she kept on talking.

"He hasn't changed his mind. He still thinks it was Harry Connelly and Clint Pepper who sold that material."

I shrugged.

"Well, I think he's probably right. Those two should have been kicked out of the agency a long time ago. They were good agents once—or so I've heard—but now, the things I hear . . ." I shook my head.

"Problem is that they've got two senators in their pocket, both of whom are on the appropriations committee that oversees our budget. The senators make sure Connelly and Pepper stay on the payroll."

I went over and sat back down in the chair. The cigarette tasted good that time of morning.

"They're here, Noah. Connelly and Pepper."

"In town?"

"Yes. And Tom got up and snuck out of bed tonight. He thinks he knows where they're staying. He told me that earlier tonight. And—"

I finished her sentence for her: "And he's drinking again."

"It's been nearly a year since he's touched a drop. But two days ago, when he heard that Connelly and Pepper were in town—he hasn't even gone to work. He just sits in this saloon and drinks. Then he staggers home and tells me what he's going to do to them. I thought that it might be just talk until tonight. But then somebody told him that Connelly and Pepper were staying at the Gladbrook. That's where he must have gone tonight."

Kansas City was filled with various types of gambling establishments, and the Gladbrook was the spot preferred by the high rollers and the rich folks. One night in a Gladbrook room cost you three or four times what it did in a hotel like mine. You paid a lot more for chefs who spoke French and a restaurant that featured a string quartet. I'd take a player piano any day.

I got up, strapped on my gun. I got my coat and pinned my badge to the lapel. I had a feeling I needed to look official that night. People are more coopera-

tive when they see a badge, and just about any badge
will do.

"I really appreciate this, Noah."

"I have to help him, Susan. I'm his hero, remember?"

She shot me a troubled smile. I held the door open
for her and soon we were in the hall and headed
down the stairs.

Chapter 2

A man in a top hat, a red silk vest, and a smile he probably practiced in front of a mirror handed out numbers to the people impatiently waiting to get into the casino. Most of these high-toned people just couldn't wait to lose their money. They filled the reception area outside the massive casino doors. They would be admitted according to the numbers the slick man in the top hat handed them.

This was where my badge was better than a bribe. I tapped it and said, "I'm here to arrest somebody."

"But you have a lovely woman with you."

"So I do. But I'm still going to arrest somebody."

The other customers didn't like me or my badge. They had a lot more money than I did, but I had my badge and they didn't think that was fair at all. This was a world of money, was it not?

Top Hat opened the double doors. The crowd behind us tried to push inside. Top Hat was harsh: "Try that again and I won't let any of you in for an hour."

The casino was an assault of talk, laughter, smoke, light from huge chandeliers, the scent of good whiskey, the noise of gambling devices clicking and clacking, blackjack dealer patter, coy serving girls pampering lustful old patriarchs, callow rich boys pampering coy serving girls, and the whispers of professional gamblers deciding which poker table looked to have the most amateurs.

Compared to the finery worn by the women and men around us, we looked like hill trash. I felt sorry for Susan. Some of the glances set upon her by the grande dames were more insulting than words could ever be. A security person stayed with us, four feet behind.

It probably took us fifteen minutes to walk around the huge room. Susan got more and more anxious. We didn't see Tom anywhere.

She stayed on my arm until we'd made a complete circle of the place. Then she broke away momentarily, looking pale. She found two straight-back chairs—the casino discouraged sitting any place but at a gambling table so they provided chairs but they made them damned uncomfortable—and half-collapsed into one of them.

In moments, she'd gone from looking wan to looking flushed.

I leaned down so I could whisper. "Are you sick?" I asked.

She put her lips next to my ear. "It's my woman's time of the month. I get chills. They're even worse than the cramps."

"I'm sorry." I started to bring my head up, then stopped: "Why don't you stay here? I'll look around some more."

Her grip was iron.

"I'm going with you."

When we had made another quarter circle of the huge room I stopped and looked back at our security guard.

"You interested in money?"

"No, I hate money. That's why I work in a casino."

"We need to find some people and fast. They may be in danger."

"Then it's casino business and I won't take money. Just tell me what you'd like me to do."

"There'll be two men together. One is Harry Connelly, the other is a man named Clint Pepper."

I described them.

"You didn't find them on the floor?"

"No. Is there a private room somewhere for high rollers?"

"I'm not at liberty to talk about anything like that. You'd need to talk to the casino manager."

"There isn't time for that. You can get in that private room a lot faster than I can. You go in there and see if they're there. If they are, tell them that Noah Ford needs to talk to them. And tell them it's urgent."

"I'll have to get permission to leave the floor."

"That's fine. But there's one more thing." I looked at Susan. "Describe Tom to him."

She did, even including the clothes he'd been wearing.

Connelly had put on some weight but he was still the urbane dandy that far too many women found appealing. Pepper had lost some weight. A casino was their natural habitat and they were turned out nicely for it in the kind of Edwardian coats, brocaded vests, and mutton-chopped sideburns favored by the prosperous city men of the day. The clothes were an affectation. They hid the truth about the men who wore them.

That night, they'd probably been playing without benefit of cheating. There were all sorts of places where you could skin rubes alive and get away with it, but in a casino like that one, cheating could be dangerous, even deadly, even though they would have been just about the only armed men in the casino. Guns were not permitted at poker tables, neither big nor small, but federal agents had a lot more freedom than most people.

Both of these men lived outside the law. They used their status as federal agents to stay free of jail cells. Crooked agents were standard ever since the war. The best spies, it had been discovered, were often pretty terrible people. But they were usually not quite as terrible as the people they were after. So they were given the chance to hide behind their badges. Agents didn't come much more terrible than Harry Connelly and Clint Pepper. Their specialties were robbery and rape. They'd broken three major cases over the past two years, though, so the powerful senators who sponsored them were adamant about keeping them in place.

"Good evening," Connelly said. He'd been with a traveling theater troupe in the West before the war. He tried to add flourish to everything he said and did. "When the security man told me that I'd get to gaze upon the beauty of Susan Daly, I of course came with great dispatch."

Pepper laughed. "Good old Harry never changes, does he?"

"I doubt you do, either, Pepper."

"Our fellow agent doesn't sound very happy to see us," Connelly said.

"Shut up and listen. Tom Daly is drinking again. He's still bitter that Washington thinks he stole those secrets. He's out tonight looking for you two. And he just might try something."

Pepper glanced at Connelly and said, "I don't know about you, Harry. But I'm positively terrified."

They were working their old familiar stage act. I'd gotten tired of it a long time ago.

"To be safe, go back to your rooms and stay there. I'll find him and get him home."

"I'd be willing to spend the night with his missus," Connelly said.

"I'd kill myself before I'd let that happen," Susan snapped.

"If I didn't know any better, Harry, I'd say neither one of these folks are glad to see us."

"Well, I warned you. That's all I can do," I said.

"You know your problem, Noah? You always think you're in charge of every situation that comes up. You're going to be worm food a lot sooner than Pepper and I will be. The day I'm afraid of some nervous little bastard like Tom Daly, I'll start wearing a dress."

He leered at Susan. "That offer still stands, Mrs. Daly. I'd be right happy to keep you company tonight."

She was even angrier than I thought. A second after she took a single step forward, a huge silver globule of spittle hung from Connelly's nose.

He couldn't help himself. He lunged for her the

way he would a man. I stepped in front of him and shoved him back at Pepper.

Pepper grabbed his arms and said, "Cool down, Harry. Any bitch who'd marry somebody like Daly isn't worth getting mad at." He smirked at her. "If I know Daly, she's still a virgin, anyway."

The security guard had seen the dustup. He came over. "Everything all right here?"

"A little disagreement, is all," I said.

"Old friends," Pepper said. "Just a little too much to drink, is all."

Connelly was still boiling. "I'll tell you one thing, Ford. If I do run into Daly and he gives me any excuse at all, this little woman here'll be pickin' out a pine box for him by sunup."

"You gave him every excuse there is to shoot if he sees Daly," Pepper said. "You warned him that Daly was stalkin' him. No court in the world'd blame Harry here for bein' scared enough to shoot first."

The guard could see that this argument wasn't going to end anytime soon. "Why don't you take the lady here and go stand on the porch in back? I'll see that these two gentlemen get a drink on the house and some more gambling. How's that sound?"

He was good at what he did. He had a job I wouldn't want. Trying to soothe people who'd just dropped a lot of money or break up fights between drunks wasn't my idea of a good time.

I took Susan's arm and started to steer her toward the back porch, which was about ten feet away.

And that was when it happened.

Just as we had turned, and presumably just as

Connelly and Pepper had turned, Tom Daly made his appearance.

He stood in the doorway of the back porch, his .45 aimed and ready to fire. "Which one of you wants it first? Connelly or Pepper?" His smile was drunken and ugly. "Get Susan out of here, Noah, so I can do my job."

Chapter 3

The bouncer froze. His instincts were obviously to rush Tom, who looked like the world's oldest altar boy in his slicked-down hair with the cowlick in back, the cheap disheveled suit, and the face that would have been adolescent if not for all the wrinkles and lines.

To the bouncer, Tom said: "Get them to turn around and then take their guns. I'll kill at least two of you if you try anything."

The bouncer's first responsibility was to see that nobody got killed. Bad enough that a drunken little man with a gun could cause a scandal in such an exalted casino. He said to me, "Is he your friend?"

"Yes."

"Then talk to him."

"No!" Tom said. "No talking. Just have them turn around and face me. And then you take their guns."

I nodded to the bouncer. At that moment there wasn't much hope of calming Tom down.

"All right you men, turn around slowly and then

hand me your guns. And let's keep everything friendly here. I'm sure we can talk to this man."

"Just stand here and let him shoot us when he wants to?" Connelly asked.

"There isn't going to be any shooting," the bouncer said.

"You going to guarantee that?" Pepper asked.

"C'mon now. We all agreed. You two turn around and then we'll talk."

The bouncer sounded a lot more confident than he looked. He was as pale as Susan and his right hand had begun to twitch, little tremor-like explosions. I was pretty sure he was coming to the conclusion that he had little or no control of the situation, the kind of moment a bouncer isn't used to.

"Now, c'mon, men. Just turn around here."

The bouncer sounded like a camp counselor pleading with bullies.

By then, we had an audience, an ever-expanding one. This would be something else the owner would not be happy about. The worst thing that could happen to a casino was when its customers were distracted away from the tables.

They turned around.

Connelly was covering his fear with jokes.

"I don't know about you, Pepper, but I sure don't want to get shot by a dwarf."

"And a drunk one at that," Pepper said.

"Shut up, you two," I said.

"Oh, oh," Connelly said, "it's the boss."

"We sure wouldn't want to make the boss mad."

"You notice how the boss is kind've standing behind the dwarf's wife there? Like if there's any shooting, he'll hide behind her."

"Well, the boss is too valuable to kill. He told me so himself."

A few people in the crowd laughed. They had to be thinking what Connelly and Pepper wanted them to think—that here were two really tough men. Even in the face of a madman holding a gun on them, they had enough presence to joke it up.

Susan took three steps toward Tom. He got a little frantic there, trying to keep his eye on Connelly and Pepper, but also to peripherally watch Susan as she approached.

"Stay there, Susan!"

"I just want to take you home, Tom. You'll feel better after you get a good night's sleep."

"We'd still be in Washington if it hadn't been for these two stealing that information and then making it look like I took it."

"They don't matter, Tom. Only you and I matter. Now please just give me the gun and let me take you home. The kids'll be so glad to see you."

"No!" he shouted. Then he raged at me. "I asked you to get her out of here, Noah. Now take her away. I'm going to get a written confession from these two because if I don't, they're going to die here tonight."

"But you'll die, too," Susan said.

"I don't care anymore, honey. I had a good record at the agency until these two messed everything up for me. I don't want my children to think I would sell government secrets. You think I want our children to grow up with that on their shoulders?"

"They wouldn't think that, Tom. They love you and they're proud of you. And they'd know the truth, no matter what anybody else said."

"All right, sir. They're ready to put their guns down."

The confusion was getting to Tom. He wasn't finished talking with Susan, which had to be good for him even under these circumstances, but he also had to watch the two men he wanted to kill.

His eyes flicked back to them and that was when I moved. It was eight steps to the porch. I eased myself around Tom—his gun couldn't cover all of us at the same time—and got myself a couple steps closer to the back porch. A heavy summer moon hung lazy in the plains sky. Somewhere a fiddler, innocent of the little drama in the casino, played a sweet sentimental song. The only thing to spoil moon and tune was the other bouncer sneaking up on Tom with a sawed-off shotgun.

He'd have killed Tom. He didn't look as if he had much interest in life, just death. Who wanted to spend all that time talking, all that time providing thrills for the onlookers who'd just turn it into dinner table chatter, anyway?

I moved. Tom saw me. There was no way I could stop that, but he had to choose between keeping me covered or keeping his gun on Pepper and Connelly.

I saw a moment of panic on his face, and then something like defeat, and then he turned away from me, bringing his gun solidly on to Connelly and Pepper.

I heard the sound of his hammer cocking, but I had no more time for Tom. I had to worry about the bouncer on the back porch who was going to try and shoot Tom in the back.

He was maybe five feet from the back door when I stepped in front of him. At that moment, I was like him. I didn't have any desire for talk, either. I hit him hard enough on the jaw to drop him to his knees. Then I hit him a second time, sending him over backward. The sawed-off I pitched off the porch.

"I'm not going to sign one damned thing," Connelly was saying.

"Then you're going to die," Tom said.

"Why don't I buy everybody a round or two of drinks and we'll sit down and try and hash it all out?"

I was beginning to like this bouncer. Even if he was just cynical, just didn't want bloodshed because of the casino's reputation, he wanted a peaceful conclusion.

I checked to see if the bouncer had taken their guns. He had. They sat together on a near table. But not near enough for Connelly and Pepper to lunge for them.

I took a deep breath and felt some of the tension leak out of me. Everything was under control by then. Everything was going to be all right. Tom was still drunk, still wanting to shoot Connelly and Pepper with that gun he was waving around, but he was talking now. The longer he talked the more he would sober up. Soon, I knew, he would start crying, and then it would all be over.

Just as long as no one started shooting first.

And then I saw him. A security man, tall, bearded, encircling Connelly and Pepper and aiming his Colt at Tom.

He was going to be the hero. He was going to be

the one written up in the newspaper stories. He was the one his lodge would be bragging about for the rest of its days.

I knew I had only a few seconds. I had to combine what I'd been planning to do with this new problem.

On my third step toward Tom, I raised my .44 and fired two quick shots at our hero, a few inches above his head. He did what I'd hoped he would do. He hit the floor for cover without even thinking of firing his gun. Suddenly, being a hero wasn't half as important as saving his ass.

Tom was just starting to turn back to me when I grabbed him and threw him down on the floor.

Though I'd been planning on holding him until the inside bouncer could get some cuffs on him, the outside bouncer changed my plans. It seemed he was sort of pissed off that I'd knocked him out and thrown his sawed-off away.

He charged at me through the doorway, his hands leading him, shaping themselves to fit my throat. He must have looked just like a bear cub when he was born because right then he appeared to be the size and power of a full-grown grizzly.

I hadn't counted on him but he hadn't counted on me, either. One thing I rarely did was just stand there when somebody was about to attack me. Somehow, that didn't seem like a very sensible thing to do.

But I did have to stand there long enough to put the point of my Texas boot straight into his groin.

He went into heavy dramatics. Falling face down, clutching his crotch, the noises of frustrated rage muffled somewhat by the fact that his mouth was about an inch from the floor.

Then I looked back to see what was going on behind me. And that was when Connelly threw a full
whiskey bottle at me, crashing against the side of my
head and momentarily sending me down into some
deep damp darkness.

Chapter 4

I wasn't out long. When I staggered to my feet, I saw that I was on the back porch along with all the others involved in Tom's standoff.

It's a terrible thing to hear a drunk cry. Susan had Tom standing against the porch railing and was talking to him in a soft voice. He was choking on his tears. I imagine he was embarrassed then. When he was sober, he wasn't a foolish man. Liquor makes us strangers, even to ourselves.

The good bouncer had Connelly and Pepper in the opposite corner. They were talking quietly, too. The bad bouncer stood nearby, glowering at me as I got all wobbly to my feet.

The casino was the casino again. The noise was that of a midnight train rushing through the night. There was laughter, chatter, the various sounds of gambling devices, and the steady drone of gamblers calling out their bets.

I walked over to Tom and Susan.

"I'm really sorry, Noah. I made another damned mess. I just wish I could let go of this thing."

"I know it's not easy for you to do but you really have to just live it out, Tom. I talk you up whenever I'm in D.C. and so do a lot of other agents."

"Really?"

"Sure, really. Hell, we know you didn't take those secrets."

Susan reached down and took his hand.

"I'd still like to see those two in prison," he said.

"You'd have to stand in line to. Everybody wants to see them in jail."

"What I can't believe is that the agency keeps them on," Susan said. "They're such scum."

"Useful scum sometimes," I said. "But they'll slip up one of these days."

"You think so?" Tom asked, unable to keep a hopeful sound out of his voice.

"Sure. They push everything. And someday those senators who promote them will have to drop 'em. They'll do something even they can't afford to be associated with."

The good bouncer came over. "Well, they've agreed not to bring in the law."

I laughed. "The kindness of their hearts?"

"They said they have to be on a train tomorrow morning early. They can't wait around for court. And nobody was seriously hurt, so I'm sure my bosses won't want to press any charges against Mr. Daly here, either."

Susan leaned over and kissed Tom's sweaty head. "Now we can just forget about this whole thing— and them. Forget it once and for all, Tom."

He lifted his head so he could see her. "And that's exactly what I'm going to do. It was like I was crazy tonight. I just couldn't think straight."

The good bouncer nodded across the way to the bad bouncer. "If I were you, Mr. Ford, I'd go through the casino when you leave. The back exit is more private, that's Larry's station, and he isn't very happy with you."

"Fine with me. I've already got a hell of a headache." To Tom and Susan I said: "Good luck, folks. I'm headed west tomorrow afternoon. The agency's setting up a regional office and that's where I'll be working out of the next year or so."

Susan took Tom's hand again. "I'm hoping they let us stay right here. This is the nicest place we've lived outside of Washington."

I'd thought of stopping to say something to Connelly and Pepper. But the bad bouncer stood too close to them. My head hurt too much for another fight.

I made my way slowly back to my hotel. I was worn out from all the tension with Susan and Tom. All I wanted now was sleep.

The lobby was empty except for the night manager. He called my name as I tried to wobble past him. I didn't need him asking me any questions about why a woman came up to my room earlier, or why I was wearing my badge.

But he surprised me. He just handed me a telegram and smirked: "Don't worry. I didn't read it."

"I guess there's a first time for everything."

I went up the stairs like an old man, slowly and leaning heavily on the railing. I was tired, but it was more than just a physical exhaustion. Dealing with

Connelly and Pepper always left me feeling dirty, and seeing Tom like that just left me weary.

The lamps were turned low in the carpeted hallway, but I didn't need much light to find my door, unlock it, and push my way in.

I heard him before I saw him, and the fact that I was moving so slowly probably saved my life. As the door swung inward, I paused for a moment, leaning against the door jamb, and heard a small grunt as the swinging door struck someone hiding in the corner.

I knew right away who it was.

Good old Fred Cartel, with his bad temper and his worse timing.

I didn't have a lot of choice. If I tried to get away, he would shoot me in the back, so I did the only thing I could think of. I dove to the floor, my gun coming into my hand, turned, and just as Fred came out from behind the door to try and shoot me I put two bullets into his shooting arm.

This was a night for drunken crying, which is what he was still doing when the local law got there and took him off to jail. The night manager of the hotel offered to clean up Fred's blood and tidy up the room but I was in too much head pain to care about messy rooms or even blood.

I had just laid my head down on the pillow when I remembered the telegram I'd forgotten to read. I did my best to make sense of it. Something about a bank robber and somebody blowing up something or other. Something about how I was needed somewhere else and fast. I slept till nearly noon and got up and reread the telegram. Then I headed west.

Chapter 5

Five Months Later

My first extended assignment was to help local law stop a bomber who was working a wide area setting off large explosions at various federal government buildings at night. Part of my job was to determine if there was a new type of explosive involved.

The first suspicion was that the man was a former Confederate soldier. The war might have ended on paper but that was the only place it had ended.

Turned out, the man was a woman and the bombings had nothing to do with the war. Her husband, a miner who had learned how to handle explosives during the war and had apparently taught his wife more than a little bit as well, had been hanged for robbing trains carrying federal government goods. She didn't believe the hanging was fair because his two partners were given long sentences. They had confessed that while they'd been along for the stealing, they hadn't approved of the killing, which, they claimed, had always been done by the husband. So she set off to protest what she saw as a great injustice. I was inclined to agree, because if the other two had been so much against the killings, why had they continued to go along on the robberies?

I spent Christmas in Denver in a whorehouse. There are some who would no doubt find that morally reprehensible, and others who would find it awful lonely-sounding. I didn't find it to be either one. There was a great turkey feast and the girls all told stories about the dopiest of their customers (making me wonder, of course, what they'd say about me), and afterward I went upstairs and had myself a good sleep, only to wake up with a very pretty young prairie girl helping me keep the bed warm. We got on right nicely, if you care to know any of the details.

On January 3, while working in the mountains with a local sheriff who was trying to find out who had killed a federal judge who had been spending the holidays with his family there, I got the telegram from Susan Daly.

TOM SENT TO WILLOW BEND ON ASSIGNMENT.
CONNELLY AND PEPPER ALSO WORKING CASE.
AM SCARED FOR TOM.
PLEASE HELP. — SUSAN

I wasn't sure I could get there in time to help. And as much as I owed him, I couldn't leave a case of this importance and take a train somewhere to talk him out of his plans.

I didn't even feel guilt about my reluctance. He'd saved my life but I'd helped him at several key times

in the past four years, especially where his drinking
was concerned.

But later in the day one of those little coincidences
that make life both interesting and frightening took
place. I got a second telegram, this one from Washington, D.C., informing me that a bank robber
named Chaney who worked out of Willow Bend had
used some explosives to blow up the back end of a
bank one night when it was empty. I sent a return
telegram, wanting to know why Connelly and Pepper
just happened to be on the same assignment. The return wire read:

FEDERAL AGENT JIM SLOANE MURDERED
WHILE INVESTIGATING ROBBERIES.
AGENT DALY SENT IN AS REPLACEMENT.
AGENTS CONNELLY AND PEPPER REQUESTED
ASSIGNMENT.

That wasn't like Connelly and Pepper. They were
rarely given the important tasks of breaking counter-
feiting rings or ferreting out plots against the government or protecting members of the judiciary, and
they certainly didn't care at all about the death of a
fellow agent. They mostly worked the lower levels of
crime. They had personal acquaintance with every
pickpocket, burglar, flimflam artist, and gunnie for
hire in the West. They knew them because they had
practiced the same esteemed callings themselves over
the years.

The fact that they'd requested this assignment—
undoubtedly after Tom had been sent there—made
me wonder if they weren't getting just a little bit tired

of all his accusations. Especially if they were true, it would be in their best interest to silence him once and for all. And where better to do that than some out-of-the-way place like Willow Bend?

I probably still wouldn't have gone to Willow Bend if we hadn't caught the break we needed in the case. The same man who'd killed the first federal judge had badly wounded a second one. But that judge had badly wounded his would-be killer in the process. The killer was in a hospital in grave condition. The wire relating all this information also said that he had confessed to the crimes and would be held until it was determined where he would be tried. There are always jurisdictional problems in cases like that but unless the second judge died, I assumed the trial would be held where the first judge lived—if the killer lived long enough to even stand trial.

And that was how I came to be in Willow Bend.

Winter had blessed the prosperous town of Willow Bend with several inches of snow, giving it the look of a sentimental holiday card.

I took a hotel room and then headed directly for the library, which was a single large room in the basement of the haberdashery. Though newspaper stories were usually slanted to the tastes and whims of the man who owned the press, looking through a few months' of weekly papers gave you a quick idea of who the powers were and what events the citizenry were interested in.

The richest man in that part of the Territory was one John Flannery Sr. Along with his other investors, he owned six banks. The newspaper owner was no friend of his. A number of stories suggested that his son, Flannery Jr., who had run the family business for the past several years, was foreclosing many ranch and farm loans in the Territory so he could sell his reclaimed property for several times its present worth to "a cabal of Eastern interests." Most of the time all that Western papers had to say was "Eastern interests" and their readers were ready to draw their guns. They didn't need "cabal."

But the Flannery family had a serious problem. Every single one of the family-owned banks had been robbed in the previous three months and—it was suspected—the money turned over to ranchers and farmers by the Robin Hood-like bank robber. It was also suspected that he may have killed a federal man who'd been out there before me.

Sheriff Nordberg was quoted as saying that he had "no proof" that a young man named Michael Chaney was the culprit, though there seemed to be a popular belief he was. Nordberg said, "There's no doubt people are treating him like a hero. They won't even consider the possibility he killed that federal man. They say he'd never kill anybody."

All this made young Flannery look bad, according to the stories. Flannery Jr. couldn't seem to stop the robberies, not even with a $10,000 reward being offered for concrete information.

None of this information had any direct bearing on Tom Daly or Connelly and Pepper, but because I would have to be asking a lot of questions of people I didn't know, it wouldn't hurt to have some sense of what was on their minds.

The rest of the material was pretty much what

you'd find in all weekly newspapers. A discussion of sanitation at a town council meeting; a belated statue to be built in the town park honoring a Civil War hero; and all the usual material about births, deaths, and potluck church suppers that filled the hours between.

Because I was a stranger, shaved and in a clean cattleman's suit and Stetson, the librarian came over every so often to see if there was any other material I needed. She had a quietly erotic face and intelligent brown eyes.

"This is some story about this Chaney. Robbing banks and giving the money to the ranchers and farmers."

She responded cautiously. "Some people think he's a hero for doing it."

"And some people don't, I take it?"

She couldn't resist smiling. "Well, the people who don't care for him are usually associated with the Flannerys in some way."

"How about this sheriff? This Nordberg? How do you think he feels about Chaney?"

She lowered her voice. "Are you a reporter or something?"

I shook my head. "Just passing through. Interesting story. I'm surprised it hasn't gotten more attention in the Territory newspapers."

"Well, Mr. Flannery Sr. owns most of them, so he plays it down. It's embarrassing. He has guards stationed everywhere but Mike gets the money anyway."

The "Mike" told me her feelings about the young bank robber.

I stood up. "Thanks for your help."

"My pleasure."

I picked up my Stetson.

Her nice brown eyes turned coy. "I still think you're a reporter of some kind."

Chapter 6

There should be a door to the past. I'd keep mine closed.

"Well, I'll be damned."

I didn't need to turn around to see who it was. I knew who it was. I'd actually been looking for him but once he was there I wanted to go somewhere else. Fast.

"You tried any of the pussy here yet, Ford? They've got some awful nice stuff."

Good old Harry Connelly.

I was walking down one of the boardwalks. It was two in the afternoon and the streets were packed with shoppers on that snowbound but warm afternoon. Most of the shoppers were women. The ones around me looked with startled displeasure at Harry. They weren't used to hearing language like Harry's, especially not bellowed that way.

He was the same Harry, dapper in Edwardian clothes, almost foppish the way his red scarf was thrown just-so across his full-length black winter coat. At the moment, he'd be carrying a variety of weapons, including the Colt strapped to his hip and, if he ran true to form, at least two other handguns and a couple knives hidden about his person. And if he ran out of weapons, he could kill you with his hands. He was especially good at ripping eyeballs out with his thumbs.

From down the main business street came the saloon sounds of laughter and player pianos. Later, a couple of the girls who pried whiskey money from the customers would take the stage and sing a couple of songs.

I'd learned a few more things about the town since I'd left the library.

Willow Bend was one of those modern Western towns. It understood that a part of commerce was sin. Thus, the town council allowed for three saloons, two just off the center of town and another down by the railroad roundhouse. It also allowed, with much greater discretion and disdain, a bawdy-house just on the east end of the town limits.

The girls had to come in once a month and get checked by one of the town docs and if there was any trouble at the house, the madam got fined, and usually pretty heavily. The girls were not allowed to spend time with any townsmen except within the confines of the house. And they were allowed into the business district only twice a week and only for two hours for each trip. A wag suggested that the town just paint all the whores bright red and be done with it.

I'd also learned that the town had suddenly become the only place where people in that part of the Territory could find the things they needed. There'd been another town thirty miles away but it had folded when the railroad had bypassed it. By then the business was there and going to stay there.

So Willow Bend was enjoying the fruits of another town's disaster and things were moving along well. Connelly was probably right about the quality of the girls. They were a specialty of the town—as Harry had just loudly reminded the ladies now on the boardwalk.

"I'll bet I can tell you why you're in town."

"You a mind reader now, Connelly?"

"No. But it seems every time Pepper and I end up in the same place as Tom Daly, you have a habit of showing up, too."

"And just why are you here, Connelly? We both know you don't care about some rich man's banks being robbed, and I doubt you even knew who Jim Sloane was."

He gave me a hard look, but didn't answer my question. "Last time, Ford," he said, "you thought you were protecting Pepper and me from your friend. Who are you here to protect this time?"

"Whichever of you needs it," I said. "I don't like to see anyone take the law into their own hands. That was one of the oaths I swore when I put on this badge. Same as you," I added.

He shook his head. "That friend of yours has already tried to kill us, and he's still shooting his mouth off about us all over the place. If something happens to him, the law'll be on our side. You just remember that, Ford."

A woman with a regal face framed perfectly by her blue bonnet passed by. Harry not only tipped his hat but gave her a small bow. She smiled, pleased. You didn't see a whole lot of bowing in a mountain town like Willow Bend.

Connelly said, "We're here to have some fun since we wrapped up that revenue case. Now Washington told us to help out the sheriff finding this Mike Chaney." He laughed. "Chaney could run for office, the kind of publicity he's getting. The thing is, he's messing with six banks that are the pride of the National Banking System. And don't forget Chaney was the guy who probably killed Sloane, the federal guy the boss sent out here before us, just like he killed Nick Tremont's boy."

"I heard that was self-defense, that Tremont drew down on him."

"Well, that's what you'd expect Chaney to say, isn't it?"

"This Flannery really foreclosing so he can sell the land to some Eastern circuit?"

Connelly made a clucking sound. "Why, I do believe you think he's doing the right thing, helping all these poor farmers and ranchers. That's why I say he could run for office, he gets any more popular. The thing you seem to forget, Ford, is that he's breaking federal law. This isn't homegrown money he's stealing; this is the real thing, money printed in Washington, D.C., and printed on government presses."

Not until after the war did the government step in and demand that the currency become federalized. Until then banks could print their own currency. Banks failed by the score and everyday people were cheated out of millions. By that point there was only one kind of currency and banks had the right to call in federal help if they were getting robbed. Connelly and Pepper would be hunting for the local Robin Hood.

"He's a banker, Ford. He makes money by investing. If these people can't pay, he has a right to foreclose."

"Some banks take the long view. They see that it's good to help local people stay in business, even if they have to float them for a while and let them pay when they can."

Connelly shook his head, pulled a gold watch from his coat pocket. "He's a banker, not a priest. Why shouldn't he make money when he can?"

"The way people seem to like this Chaney around here, it might cost him a lot of business. They might go somewhere else."

"That's where John is sitting pretty," he laughed. "There's no other bank within sixty miles of here."

Chapter 7

"This is getting to be a convention," Sheriff Daryl Nordberg laughed after I had introduced myself and taken the chair he'd offered me. "I can't remember ever having this many federal agents here at the same time."

"I'm here unofficially."

He was square. Square head; big, square shoulders; wide, square hands. The blue Swedish eyes were friendly enough but the mouth hinted that the friendliness could disappear fast. He wore a khaki uniform. Despite his thinning hair, he looked no older than midtwenties to me.

The office was also square. Two pine filing cabinets, a glassed wall case holding three different types of rifles, and a four-shelf bookcase behind him. There were three photographs of the same pretty young woman. In one of the photographs, he stood close enough to her to have his arm around her shoulders.

"I guess I don't know what you mean by unofficial."

"Connelly and Pepper have an argument with the other agent, the one who came to replace Jim Sloane and to find out how he died. I'm worried that something might happen. I want to get to the agent before anything does."

Blond eyebrow raised. "Connelly and Pepper, you say?"

I nodded.

"There's a pair of characters for you. They dress like some kind of theater boy."

"It's an act."

He nodded, looked unhappy. "I found that out. Somebody said something to one of them in a saloon here the other night and Pepper broke his nose and knocked out three of his teeth. And the woman who runs the whorehouse said there's no doubt they like the ladies."

"They're tough boys. But I want to keep them away from Tom Daly. You got a handle on folks who come through town?"

"If Daly's a little guy with a big mouth, I can tell you right where to find him."

"That doesn't sound good."

He leaned back in his office chair. It needed some grease. "Nothing big. Nothing even worth running him in for. But he's been here about a week and he's already been kicked out of two boardinghouses."

"You happen to know where I'd find him now?"

"As of yesterday, he was staying with a woman named Emma Landers. She's a widow lady who runs a boardinghouse for railroad men. I asked her to take him." He smiled. "I'm a chicken. Scares me to run a federal man in, even if he is a drunk. I've got a wife and a baby to support."

I looked again at the photographs behind him.

Wife in all three; him in one. But no evidence of a child.

"I won't get you involved unless I need to. Sounds like you've got a lot to do already with this Mike Chaney."

"I've got two part-time deputies looking for him now. Plus Connelly and Pepper. No luck so far."

"How about a full-out manhunt?"

He shook his head. "For one thing, Western Union told me that there are a lot of bad storms headed this way. I don't know if you've ever seen a mountain storm before, but it's about the most dangerous thing I can think of. You get caught in an avalanche, you probably won't survive. I don't want to have a lot of men caught out there in that. And for another—" He paused. "He's a hero to a lot of people who wouldn't have ranches and farms today if he hadn't robbed those banks."

"And this Flannery Jr. is the villain?"

He frowned. "He's a businessman. He has a chance to make a lot of money selling land that people can't pay for. He's within his rights."

"So he hasn't done anything illegal?"

"If you mean has he burned them out or run their cattle off or cut off access to water—all the things you usually hear about—no. He's scared of failing his old man. That's what it comes down to. I don't know if Junior would do all this if his old man didn't expect him to. A lot of people who inherit businesses do a damned good job with them. I think the ones who don't live up to their fathers are probably in the minority. Right here in the valley we've got three businesses run by Juniors. And they all do fine."

"Tell me about Flannery Jr."

"Little bit of a bully. Ladies' man, too, though Mike Chaney's that also. And he's got a personal grudge against Chaney."

"What would that be?"

"A young woman that they both wanted to marry. Flannery married her but the gossip is she isn't happy and thinks maybe she should have married Chaney. And now Chaney's robbing all Junior's banks and getting away with it."

"Maybe Junior deserves it."

He laughed. "You sound like you've thrown in with the others, Ford."

That was when I heard footsteps slapping the floor on their way back there. The deputy who sat out front said, "Nolan's here. He thinks he spotted Mike Chaney about an hour ago up near Indian Nook Pass. Nolan's out back with his horse."

Nordberg exploded from his chair. "You'll excuse me, Mr. Ford. I need to take care of this."

He didn't wait for me to say anything.

I slipped on my Stetson, shifted my gunbelt to a more comfortable position, and then walked to the front where a young woman sat.

She was a tall, slim woman of about twenty-two. The dark eyes gave the classical face a forlorn look.

She was reading but lowered the magazine when I came out. I hadn't noticed her anxiety until she spoke in a trembling voice: "Did they find Mike?"

"The deputy said somebody named Nolan thought he saw him up somewhere near Indian Nook Pass."

She took a very deep, obvious breath as if to bring herself under tighter control. I waited for her to say something but then she didn't.

The front door opened and a man who looked as if he wouldn't mind beating somebody to death—fists were a lot more personal than six-shooters—came in and stamped snow off his feet.

"Good evening, Mr. Tremont."

"Good evening, Mrs. Flannery," he said in a tight voice that didn't sound all that friendly.

"How's your wife doing?" she asked.

"She'll be a lot happier when we find Chaney and make him stand trial for killing our boy."

I decided that would be a good time to leave. The woman put her eyes back on the magazine. Mr. Tremont just stood there and seethed.

But I couldn't get out the door just yet, either. A small woman with a freckled, pretty face came in carrying an infant wrapped in several baby blankets. The infant was done up like a mummy, not that you could blame the woman. Not in weather like that.

"Evening, Mrs. Nordberg," the woman with the magazine said pleasantly.

The sheriff's wife smiled nervously. "I just stopped in to see if my husband was busy. I can see that he is. I'll just see him at home."

The woman brought out the gentleman in Tremont. He doffed his bear fur hat and said, "Evening to you, ma'am."

Then she was gone. And so was I, soon after.

Chapter 8

Emma Landers's house was a two-story adobe affair with two swings and several chairs on the front porch. But winter had given them all the look of orphans. Nobody would be swinging that day.

A stout woman with a pair of thick eyeglasses came to the door shooting the sleeves of her faded gingham dress.

"All filled up, mister. Sorry."

"I'm looking for Tom Daly."

"So am I." She didn't sound happy when she said it. "You see him, tell him he owes me money for the glasses he broke last night." Her gray hair stuck straight up in jagged pieces. She was in need of a comb. But I doubted she cared. "I told him to leave the glasses alone, I'd carry them to the kitchen. He was too drunk to carry 'em and I told him so. But he wouldn't listen. Oh, no, he was perfectly fine to carry them. There wouldn't be any trouble at all. So what does he do? He trips over his own feet and breaks every single one of them. Ordered them from Sears. They weren't even three weeks old. I had to go shopping this morning so I wasn't here when he woke up. I can imagine the hangover he had. Anyway, if he remembers what he did he's probably too scared to come back."

She shook her head. "You know what's the worst of it? You never met a nicer little feller in your life when he's sober. But you got to catch him before eight o'clock at night because afterward—"

"Well, I'll stop back then, ma'am."

"Before eight."

"Before eight."

I started to walk away.

"I say who stopped by?"

"No, that's all right. I'll just see him later."

I had a piece of chicken and a baked potato with butter just after one o'clock that afternoon. The businessmen were just starting to leave, heading back to their stores.

The woman from the jail came up and sat next to me at the counter.

"You're Mr. Noah Ford?"

"I am."

"My name is Laura Flannery. I saw you in the sheriff's office a while ago. Do you remember?"

"Now how could I forget such a fine-looking woman in such a short amount of time?"

She had a sweet melancholy girl voice, the sort you could almost listen to if she was just reading a list of names.

"Deputy Rolins told me that you're a federal agent."

"Yes."

"But you're not with the other two."

"No, I'm not."

The woman behind the counter was pretending to arrange several loaves of bread to build them into a kind of presentation. What she was really doing was eavesdropping.

"Feel like taking a walk?"

She touched my sleeve.

Whispered: "Thank you."

The warm day was now a cold one. Above the Rockies, ancient serpents in the form of dark clouds slithered across the gray sky, coiling and uncoiling and seeming to wrap themselves around the jagged tops of mountains.

The people in the streets responded the way forest animals would. They moved a little faster, watched the sky furtively, bent their heads to the increasing wind.

"Storms scare me," Laura Flannery said as we moved along the street. "When I was little, I used to hide in the closet until they were over. I guess it was the wind more than anything. I still don't like the sound of it when it comes down from the mountains the way it's starting to now."

"Probably be a bad one," I said. I wondered what was on her mind.

"You could get me into a lot of trouble if you repeat what I ask you to do."

"Oh? How would that be?"

"I want you to bring Mike Chaney in."

Chaney and John Flannery had fought over her. She had married Flannery. Now she was asking me to bring Chaney in.

"Those two will kill him. They had supper at our house last night. They're terrible men. I hope you'll forgive me for saying that."

"I'm afraid that it's their assignment. I'm in town on another matter. I can talk to them but they're in charge of the Chaney case."

"Will they listen to you? I got the impression that they didn't like you very much. I'm sort of surprised to see men like that working for the government."

"They have their uses. They've done some good work."

She laughed. "You're quite the diplomat. Aren't you just churning inside to tell me what trash they are?"

I smiled. " 'Churning' is a little strong."

"Then you don't like them, either."

"As I say, they have their uses."

In a whisper almost lost to the wind, she said: "Damn."

I didn't need an introduction to know who he was. He wasn't a showboat but he did have the stride of the overboss, the plantation manager, the man in charge of the chain gang. He wore a black bowler, which he barely kept on his head in the wind and a long, expensive black coat. He was more handsome than he needed to be and when he saw us, he put on a smile that a politician would envy—big and empty.

"Well, I see my wife has a new friend," he said. It was one of those statements that had a whole lot of troubled history in it.

"Mr. Ford, this is my husband, John. John, Mr. Ford is a federal agent."

"Oh, yes, Mr. Ford. Your associates were telling me all about you last night."

I gave him my own fake smile right back. "Don't believe everything you hear."

"I'm sure my wife told you all about our supper last night. I'm afraid she wasn't taken with them. But she seems to find you just about right."

The implication of that made her blush.

"Was she asking you to spare Mike's life? She wouldn't let go of that subject last night. That's why she doesn't like them, of course. Afraid they'll kill the town hero—even though he's stealing from the bank that puts the food on our table."

He extended a gloved hand and we shook.

"I have to get back to work. It's nice to meet you, Mr. Ford." And then he winked at me, making sure his wife saw it. "Have her home by dark, otherwise I might get suspicious."

His smile back in place, he walked on down the street.

I wasn't quite sure what to say.

"Maybe I'd better get home," she said. Easy to see that she was embarrassed by how he'd treated her. Her eyes gleamed with tears. He'd just beaten her up pretty badly. He was smart enough to use words instead of fists. Looks bad when the wife of the bank president is all black and blue. She started away and then turned back to me and said: "John really wants to see somebody kill Mike."

Then she was gone.

Chapter 9

"What the hell do you want, Ford?"

"I'm going to ruin your day for you, Harry. You too, Pepper."

He laughed. "Sit down and have a beer."

Clint Pepper said, "I saw you talking to Flannery's wife. She's one nice piece of tail."

"She's going to kill him someday, though," Connelly said. "You know how you read in the papers sometimes a wife goes crazy and shoots her husband? I almost thought she was going to do that last night."

"Yeah, I heard you had dinner at their place," I said. "Heard you said a lot of nice things about me."

The name of the saloon was Thirsty. We were probably the only people in the place who weren't talking about the coming storm.

Connelly had two schooners of beer in front of him. Saved him a trip to the bar for the next one.

He shoved one over to me. "Drink up. And I wasn't the one running you down, Noah. You know me better than that. I love you like a brother. It was Pepper here. He was the one doing the dirt."

Pepper, the dapper master of the sneer, said, "I admit it, Ford. I'd had too much to drink and actually heard myself say a few unkind things about you."

"Downright uncharitable things," Connelly said.

"The first thing this morning, guess what I did?" Pepper asked. "I went straight to church and asked the priest to hear my confession. I told him that I had said several terrible things about the great Noah Ford."

"And Clint here's not even a Catholic."

I shoved my beer back at Connelly and let them have their laugh. When they were done amusing themselves, I said: "I don't drink alcohol anymore."

"You're a regular altar boy," Connelly said.

"I have a letter back in my office in D.C. from a man named Milt Seltzer. And you know what it says?"

Nothing dramatic happened. They didn't glance at each other and start acting nervous. But Pepper did gulp and Connelly got that tic in his eye that came when pressure was suddenly put on him.

"Mr. Seltzer says that he's willing to testify in a court of law that two federal agents named Connelly and Pepper who were supposed to be investigating the murder of a federal judge—who just happened to be Mr. Seltzer's brother—these two agents took a bribe to change the findings of their investigation and conclude that the killer was still unknown. Mr. Seltzer hired a Pink to investigate and the Pink got the wife of the killer to swear to the fact that he had murdered the judge because of a court ruling and that he paid these agents off to file a false report. Now that's something that not even a United States senator could protect a federal agent from. Now I haven't quite decided how to handle this letter. Maybe it's something the boss should see."

Pepper said, "You always were quite the yarn-spinner, Ford."

Connelly said, "You should be a writer, you're so good at yarn-spinning, Ford."

"So you wouldn't mind if I wired Washington and told the boss where he could find the letter in my desk?"

This time they did glance at each other. This time they did look a little nervous.

"How would you have happened to come by a letter like that?" Pepper asked.

"I happened to have worked with that judge once. He was a fine man. His brother remembered me."

A pair like this, they always had to have in the backs of their minds the fear that someday, some way, something they did, something they had probably put clean out of their minds, would come back on them.

And there it was.

I didn't have any letter. I hadn't known that particular judge. But another agent, who had done follow-up on the case, had told me his suspicions. Those suspicions were coming in damn handy.

They were putting on another show for me. Anybody who knew anything about these two knew that they rarely took prisoners. If it was a woman involved, they raped her before they killed her. And if it was a man, they humiliated him before they killed him.

"I know you boys are going after Chaney. I just want to make sure he comes back alive."

"Nobody said anything about killing this Chaney, anyway," Connelly said.

"Most folks around here think he's a hero," Pepper said.

"We'd be in deep shit, we killed somebody like him. Everybody here looks up to him," Connelly said. "I don't see any reason he couldn't be brought back peaceful as all hell, do you, Pepper?"

Pepper laughed. "See, Ford here looks happy already."

"I just wanted to make sure we had an understanding," I said.

"Hell, yes, we have an understanding," Connelly said.

"We've got understanding up the ass."

I stood up. "I guess I'll hold off on sending that telegram to the boss."

I was pretty sure I saw the moose head above the bar wink at me as I passed it on my way out.

Chapter 10

I was walking through the tiny lobby of my hotel when somebody behind a newspaper said, "Noah. Over here."

Blue eyes peered over the top of the paper. I hadn't come to Tom Daly; he'd come to me.

About four feet from him the smell became familiar. He had always used the same kind of slick stuff on his thinning hair. That, combined with the smell of the rye he preferred, gave off an unmistakable aroma.

I sat in the leather chair next to him. "These are nice digs, Noah."

Men who drink the way Daly did are never quite sober. Even after a couple of days off the bottle, you see a faint trembling in their fingers and whiskey sorrow in their eyes. Even the big, loud drunks who always seem to be having such a great time when they're up there—in their rooms in the hangover mornings they're scared, confused, stomach-sick little children who ache to stop but can't.

"There's a train out of here at six tonight, Tom."

"Not in this weather there won't be."

"The storm hasn't hit yet."

"The direction that train's coming, the storm's already there. There won't be a train along for a couple days now."

"You been hanging out at the depot, have you?"

Then he surprised me. "I checked it out, yeah."

"You going back?"

He put the paper down, folded it in half, laid it carefully on the stand next to him. Even half-sober, he was a fastidious little man.

"I wired Susan. Told her I was coming home."

"I'll be damned," I said. "So Tom Daly has finally come to his senses."

"Maybe it's not what you think, Noah."

"I guess I don't follow you. You're going home, right?"

"Yeah, I'm going home. But I'm going home with something I stole from one of Pepper's bags in his hotel room."

The whiskey and the years had caught up with him. There in the sunlight-robbed lobby, sitting among the smells of stale cigars and dusty carpet, he looked small and old and finished.

"You know what I took?"

"This could be dangerous, Tom."

"Yeah, dangerous for them. I took his bank statement from this bank over in Maryland. You should see it, Noah. He's been on the take for years. The deposits are as much as two thousand dollars at a time. You know how we've always heard they were in the blackmail business? Well, this proves it. This is better than shooting them. This means a long time in prison, Noah. And you know what else? I'll bet I can talk the D.A. back there into getting them to admit they took the information the boss thinks I took." The whiskey-wasted little fellow sat up straight, grinned and said in the happiest voice I'd heard him use in years: "They go to prison and I get my name cleared. I should've thought of this a long time ago."

It made sense. The D.C. police and D.A. weren't going to worry about how he got Pepper's bank statement. All they'd care about was that it was authentic and that they could use it to show a jury that no rank-and-file federal agent could make that kind of money and still be honest. You didn't become a federal man to get rich.

"You wanna go have a drink with me and celebrate?"

"Why don't you celebrate by not taking a drink, Tom?"

"You would've made a hell of a good priest," he laughed.

"Tell you what I will do, though. How about having supper? There's that café down the street. I see they're advertising Swiss steak in the window for tonight."

"That sounds pretty damned good."

He stood up before I did. Now that he'd told me about the bank statement, his demeanor had changed. He wasn't some exultant braying fool. But damned if he didn't look a few years younger and a lot less ashen; and damned if he didn't have that old-Tom smile on him.

I cuffed him on the shoulder. "See you at five."

Chapter 11

Tom didn't make it to the café. You know enough drunks, you know that at least 50 percent of the time they don't keep their word.

I gave him twenty minutes and then went ahead and ate without him. Swiss steak and mashed potatoes wasn't the kind of meal I expected in a mountain town but I was glad to get it.

I figured the café had about half again as many customers as it could handle. There were cowboys, workers, day laborers, drummers of every description, and a few folks who felt they were too far away from their ranches and farms to risk traveling. The smoke from cigarettes, cigars, pipes, and the grill put a fog-heavy haze across everything. And every single syllable uttered seemed to be about the weather, a subject I was thoroughly sick of hearing about.

Tom had been right about the train, anyway. We wouldn't be getting out of there for a few days. And if the mountain passes got bad, I might not make it back to Denver for a week or more.

The man next to me got up from his counter seat

and another man took his place. We didn't look at each other or speak. He ordered the Swiss steak and got his coffee fast from a sweaty and desperate waitress. She deserved a few days off after that night.

I had a piece of apple pie. I ate it in gulps. I wanted out of there. That press of people plus the smoke was starting to make me tense. I'm not much for crowds. I've seen a few of them turn on people and it's always ugly. I've never seen a lynching but I have seen a crowd beat and stomp a man very close to death while six drunks held me so I couldn't go to his rescue. Later on that night, in back of a saloon, I decided for no particular reason to kill the man who'd stirred up the crowd. Like most competent lawmen, I knew how to plant a gun so it looked like self-defense.

The man next to me at the counter said, "If you go after Mike Chaney, mister, I want to go with you. Name's Jeremy Long." He offered a massive hand and I took it. "I just want to see his face when we bring him in. Thinks he's the big hero."

Even with the din, Long's voice was loud and angry. He was a fleshy man, short, balding, middle-aged, wearing a sheepskin over his work shirt. I don't suppose he was all that tough when something personal wasn't driving him. But there was obviously something between Chaney and himself that made him dangerous.

"I won't be going after him, Mr. Long. Once the trains can run again, I'm leaving town."

"Kip over to the sheriff's office told me you was a federal man."

"I am. But I'm not in town because of Chaney."

He just watched me the way a human watches a type of animal he's never seen before.

"Why ain't you after Chaney?"

"I'm working on a different case."

"You know what he done?"

"From what I hear, he robbed a bank."

He sneered. "Oh, he done a lot more than that, mister. A whole lot more than that. One of the banks he stuck up—one of Flannery's banks, of course— Flannery fired one of the clerks. Blamed him for not putting up a fight when Chaney robbed the place. Even kind of hinted around that the clerk might be in cahoots with Chaney. You know how old that clerk is? I'll tell ya. He's twenty-three. You know how many little ones he's got runnin' around? I'll tell ya that, too. He's got six little ones runnin' around. And you know what else? He's got a sickly wife, to boot. Can't do about half the work she should; and even then she's got these spells when she can't do nothing at all. And so this here clerk I've been telling you about, now he ain't got a job on top of everything else. And it's all because of the big hero, Mike Chaney."

Maybe I would have been more sympathetic if he hadn't been spitting all over me as he worked his way through his moist rage. I took out my handkerchief and wiped my face.

"I just want to see his face when they put the hand-cuffs on him. Or when they kill him. Shoot him down. Because you know he don't really care about the people he gives this money to. All he cares about is playin' the big man to everybody. 'Here I am. I'm Mike Chaney. I'm a hero.' "

Everybody was packed so tight at the counter that I kind of had to wriggle my way up out of the seat.

"I take it that clerk was your son."

"You take it right, mister."

His plight was one that most people never think about. You take any major crime like a bank robbery. It affects a whole lot of people, people you never think about. That man's son, for instance, and his sick wife. And their kids.

"I wish I could help you, mister. But I'm afraid I can't."

Somebody was in my seat within six seconds of my lifting my ass off it.

Chapter 12

I decided to try the boardinghouse where Tom Daly was staying. Or at least had been staying unless he'd managed to get himself kicked out.

When I passed by the sheriff's office I saw Nordberg talking to his wife. Even in faded blue gingham she was as pretty as a mountain sunset. The woman in the photographs in his office. She had a buffalo wrap over her shoulders. She carried her infant tight in her arms. Given the raw wind, she had to keep it completely covered.

Close up, the woman was even prettier, a delicate female face with blue eyes that spoke of intelligence but also anxiety.

"I need to talk to this man, Wendy. I'll see you in an hour or so."

"Supper's ready and waiting."

But Nordberg seemed more interested in talking to me than he did in talking to his wife. He just looked at her and said, "This is Noah Ford. This is Wendy. My wife."

She said all the nice things, including, "I hope you enjoy your stay here, Mr. Ford."

After his wife and baby were gone, Nordberg said, "C'mon inside. It's too cold to stand out here for very long."

The front desk wasn't manned. A coffeepot bubbled on the potbellied stove. He set us up with a cup each. He sat on the edge of the desk, I sat in a chair. The walls were covered with various plaques and awards his office had received. From what I'd seen of him, he probably deserved all of them.

"Your friend's at it again. He somehow met Mike Chaney's sister Jen and got her all stirred up. She was cooperating with me. But not since she's talked to Daly. And that's just one thing. About an hour ago somebody swore they spotted Chaney in town here. Not far from Jen's place. I ran out there but didn't find him anyplace. Thought I'd look around some more. I'm headed out there now. I just wanted to put something warm in my gut because I just might be outside for a long time tonight. I was going to look you up, anyway. See if you wanted to go along. After I find him, I'm going to put your friend Daly in a cell and he stays there until the train is ready to pull out and I put him on it."

"I don't blame you. I wonder how the hell he got mixed up with Chaney's sister."

"She's a very nice gal. She's just afraid that your two federal men are going to kill her brother. She's sure that Flannery Jr. put them up to it."

We took our last sips of coffee and headed out.

Chapter 13

Bone-cold, wind-whipped, wind-blinded, we spent a good (well, bad actually) two hours chasing phantoms on the north edge of town where there were ample hiding places, including a shallow wooded area, a roundhouse and boxcars, a wide creek with steep banks, and Jen Chaney's small farm.

The year I worked for the Pinkertons I did a lot of railroad investigations. I'd forgotten the dubious pleasures of scrambling up boxcars and then walking along the top while the wind was doing everything it could to hurl you to the ground and smash your bones.

Nothing.

None of the men in the roundhouse were any help, either. They had everything battened down for the big storm. I counted two card games, one penny-pitching game, and a noisy arm-wrestling match among the leisure activities. The pipe tobacco and the coffee smelled damned good on a night like that. I hated to go back outside.

There had been four of us looking—two deputies

had met us on our way out there—and since I hadn't heard any sudden shouts I guessed they'd done as poorly as I had.

The moon was a mean one. So icy-looking it made you even colder. But it showed everything up pretty good, which was bad for people trying to elude the law.

The deputy named Dob—I can't remember his last name—came tripping and stumbling and swearing and shouting and waving toward me. He was so out of breath when we caught up with each other, he put his hands on his knees and just held them there while his breathing threatened to rip his whole chest cavity apart. He sounded like a dog dying mean.

And then he said, "Your friend, Mr. Ford."

"Daly? What about him?"

He held up a hand. His panting wasn't done. It almost sounded fatal then. His nose was running and the snot glowed green in the moonlight. His white face was raw red from the wind.

"Dead."

"What?"

"Dead. And I seen who killed him."

"Who?"

More ragged breathing. "Mike. Chaney."

"Chaney? Why the hell would Chaney kill Daly?"

He just shook his head.

By now Nordberg and the other deputy were running toward us. They must have heard Dob there despite the wind.

When they reached us, Dob, in torrents of breath, told them what he'd seen and we immediately set off.

Next to the railroad tracks, Tom Daly lay face down while the wind played wild with his hair and clothes.

I knelt down next to him on the off chance that he might still be alive. But I knew better.

"And you're sure it was Chaney?" Nordberg asked. Then he said what I'd said: "Why the hell would Mike kill Daly?"

My knees cracked as I stood up. I had snot on my face now, too. I wiped the back of my glove across my nose.

I had a mental picture of Susan opening the telegram I'd have to send her. The one telling her about her dead husband. She wasn't the type who would scream or be dramatic in any way. She'd take the telegram and sit slowly down on a chair and then she'd lean her head back and close her eyes. And after a minute or two of absolute stillness, the lamplight would glisten on the soft slow tears making their way down her cheeks. There would be sobbing but that would come much later on.

"Dob, you sure you couldn't have made a mistake?" Nordberg was asking.

"No, sir. The wind blew his cap off. I got a good look at him. It was Mike Chaney for sure."

"Mike Chaney," Nordberg said, shaking his head encased in his buffalo parka hood. "Why the hell would he want to kill Daly?"

He took his turn with the corpse. While he did that, I looked around everywhere for anything that might have been dropped on the ground. A couple of moonlit glints got me curious but they both turned out to be just rocks that had that fool's-gold brilliance to them.

Nordberg came over to me and said, "You can bet that's where he went."

He pointed to the mountains. They had never looked larger or more imposing or more impregnable.

"No sense going after him tonight. He'll go high enough to get a good hiding place. We'll wait for sunup." He shook his head. "Now I got to go tell Jen." He pinched his lips together before speaking. "This just isn't like Mike Chaney."

He turned to his deputies. "One of you stay with the body and one of you go to town and get the funeral wagon out here."

He turned back to me. "I'd appreciate it if you'd come along. This isn't anything I'm up to alone."

Chapter 14

The gray hair misled me. Chaney's sister was outside the small house, scraping frost off the front window that was golden thanks to the lamp inside.

When she turned around at hearing our footsteps, the face was so young I wondered if she was wearing a gray wig.

She wore a sheepskin coat, gloves. In the lamplight, the cherry-tinted cold cheeks looked like those of a youngster building a snowman. You couldn't say she was a beauty but there was a vivid quality to her face that was almost better than beauty. The dark eyes were especially alert and alive, even in the face-battering wind.

She waited for us. She didn't step forward even an inch. The way she held herself, so rigid, it was as if she knew it was bad and was preparing herself for news that would be like a physical assault.

"Evening, Jen," Nordberg said. He sounded tense. He hadn't been exaggerating about needing moral support.

She nodded, said nothing, looked at me briefly, then back to him.

"We go inside?"

Since the sheriff hadn't said anything about her being a mute, I assumed she could talk. But she sure was spare with her words. She led us inside to a home that was as spare with furnishings as she was with words. There was a formidable four-shelf bookcase packed with various sizes of books, a horsehair couch, and a pair of rocking chairs with Indian blankets over the backs of them.

She served us coffee. She took the couch. We took the chairs. We'd been as silent as she was.

"Jen, I'm afraid I might have some—"

"Just say it, Sheriff. Did those two federal men kill him?"

"No. He isn't dead, Jen."

She had taken her coat off. She wore a black flannel shirt and dungarees. The stiffness went out of her body as the sigh escaped her lips.

"He isn't dead, but somebody else is."

"I don't understand."

"There was another man killed tonight, Tom Daly." He pointed to me. "This is Noah Ford, a federal man who's helping me." He paused. "My deputy claims he saw Mike running away from the dead man tonight."

She glanced at me and then back at Nordberg. Her face held me. There was that prairie woman sweetness mixed with that prairie woman hardness. She'd be sweet or hard depending on the circumstances.

"Mike isn't a killer."

"Well, not normally—" Nordberg obviously realized he'd put it wrong.

"Sheriff, are you trying to tell me that you seriously think Mike killed Tom Daly?"

"I'm just telling you what I know so far." He sounded apologetic, almost embarrassed.

"Tom Daly was trying to help us. He came out here and introduced himself and tried to warn me about that pair—what's their names?—Connelly and Pepper. He said that he was going to have Mr. Ford here come and talk to me, too. He wanted to make sure that if they went looking for Mike up in the mountains that Mr. Ford would be along. He said he was going to meet him at the café and ask him to do it."

Nordberg set his coffee cup down on the wooden floor. "I have to ask you some questions, Jen."

She put her hand to her forehead as if she suddenly had a bad headache. Her body sagged now. "You're going to ask me if he's here, aren't you?"

"Yes. I have to, Jen."

"Well, he isn't."

"When's the last time you saw him?"

Just then the wind kicked up hard. Easy to imagine a little box of a house like that being picked up and tumbled along the flats as if caught up in a tornado. The entire house shook.

"About an hour and a half ago."

Nordberg sighed. "By rights, you should have told him to turn himself in."

"I tried. Tom Daly was getting him some supplies from the general store and they were going to meet after the supper hour. I can't buy supplies because everybody'd know who I was getting them for."

"How long was Mike here?"

"Not long. Maybe half an hour. He stayed in the shed in the back. Most of the time he talked to Tom."

"You think he headed into the mountains?"

"Wouldn't you?" she snapped. "Everybody thinking that you murdered somebody? Wouldn't you head for the mountains?"

"I need to go out and look around. See if he might be hiding."

"I remember the day when my word was good enough." She shook her head. "When Mike's word was good enough."

"It's different now, Jen. It's murder."

"You don't know he did it."

"No, I don't. But I have to do my job." He picked up his Stetson from the floor. "I'm just doing my job here, Jen," he said again.

"You think Mr. Ford could stay and talk to me while you're looking around?"

I'd been about to stand up.

"That all right with you?" he asked.

"Sure."

He nodded to us and then walked to the door. He had to push hard on it to get it closed tight.

The wind came wicked against the front window. She looked up as if someone had knocked on her front door.

"Maybe my prayers'll be answered."

"Wind?"

"Wind and snow. The kind of blizzard that'll keep those bounty men from going into the mountains."

"Daly was a good man."

"He said the same thing about you. Said not to judge federal men by those other two."

"Connelly and Pepper."

"I can't seem to remember their names. Probably because I even hate to say them out loud." Then: "They'll go after Mike in the morning, won't they?"

"Yeah. If the weather allows it."

She folded her hands in a kind of prayerful way. Said nothing. Then: "They'll kill him now, won't they?" She didn't look up at me.

"Not necessarily."

Now she looked up. "You don't need to lie to me, Mr. Ford. Right now I'm sort of weak because I just heard about Tom Daly. But I'm strong. I know what they'll be up to tomorrow. Flannery wants him dead and Flannery always gets his way around here."

"His wife was friendly with Mike before she married Flannery? Is that how it works?"

She actually laughed. "Well, that's a very delicate way to put it. 'Was friendly.' My brother is such a tomcat he was denounced from the altar of the Methodist church one Sunday morning. Not by name, but everybody knew who he was talking about. And I'm not making any excuses for Mike, either. He'd see married women if there weren't any single women around. He even came between me and my best friend, Loretta DeMeer. I was uncomfortable when she started seeing him. Neither of them told me. Loretta and I don't speak much anymore. He isn't a saint by a long shot. So, yes, the short answer to your question is, there is still plenty of tension between Flannery and my brother. Mike wouldn't ever admit it but he may still have been seeing Laura once in a while on the sly."

I remembered the hard harsh way Flannery had treated his wife, and right in front of me. You push on a woman that way, she just might push back sometime.

A frown on that vivid, pretty face.

"Laura—this is a terrible thing to say, and you probably won't like me after I say it—but most people can't see past that beautiful face of hers. They think she's this innocent little woman. But the way she went back and forth between Mike and Flannery—

"I even felt sorry for Flannery. In the beginning, anyway. Before he got so hateful about Mike and Laura being together. But a lot of it was her fault. She wanted his money but she didn't want him. And she wanted Mike but she didn't want to live on a farm. That was his big dream. Having a farm. So she went back and forth between them. She could never quite let go of Flannery. So Mike finally just walked away from her. Wouldn't have anything to do with her. She used to come here and sit where you're sitting and cry her eyes out. She wanted me to help her get Mike back. But he wouldn't go back. And then he started seeing a lot of other women. Then she finally married Flannery."

"Did Flannery and Mike ever have it out?"

"No. I was afraid Flannery might hire somebody to beat up on Mike. He's been known to do that before."

I finished my coffee.

"So you think Laura really loves Mike?"

"Yes. That's the funny thing. She does love him. But then she looks at Flannery's mansion and fancy carriages and his trips to Europe—any woman could get her head turned that way."

"You could?"

She had a nice gentle smile.

"Not me, but Flannery's a nice-looking man. And he can be very charming."

The wind washed again against the window; invisible tide storming in. After it spent itself, she said: "Some people think Mike's a killer. But this is where I'm going to start telling you about all the good things he's done in his life. The people he's helped. How he never started a fight. I'm not saying he wouldn't fight back and give as good as he got—or better. But I'm just about positive he never started a fight in his life. And the only gun he owned was an old rifle that belonged to our dad. And Mike only used it when he went hunting, when times were lean and we needed meat for the table."

"Never owned any other kind of firearm?"

"Never."

"Then he doesn't have one up there in the mountains?"

She set her jaw. The start of anger was in those eyes. Intelligent dark eyes.

"Yeah, he has one up there. I bought him a Navy Colt and a Winchester last week when Connelly and Pepper came to town." The flash anger again. "Are you trying to tell me you wouldn't be armed in a situation like that?"

"I'm not saying anything at all, Jen. I'm just trying to understand the situation here."

"If I had any money, I'd pay you to go tomorrow morning in the mountains."

I'd been thinking about that. But instead of answering her directly, I said, "Do you have any idea where your brother might hide tonight?"

"I don't. But I know somebody who does. An old man named Chuck Gage. His shed is right behind the Lutheran church. He works there and they give him meals and the shed. My brother went to see him tonight. Chuck knows the mountains better than anybody in the valley."

Nordberg was on the steps outside.

She said: "You go visit Chuck by yourself. Don't say anything to the sheriff."

Nordberg came inside and said, "Well, if he's around here, I couldn't find him. You about ready to go, Mr. Ford?"

The rocker creaked as I left it. I'd gotten pretty comfortable sitting in it.

"You see him, Jen, you're bound by the law to tell me."

"I know."

"I know you won't." He smiled at her. "But I have to say things like that so I'll remember I'm a sheriff."

She came over to us and said, "I would tell you, Sheriff. Now I would. I don't want those federal men to get him. They'll kill him."

I thought of the deal I'd made with them. They wouldn't kill him and I wouldn't turn in a letter that didn't exist. They wouldn't have any trouble killing me if they didn't want that letter to find its way into my boss's hands. If it existed.

She gave me a look that said we shared a secret named Chuck Gage. I nodded to her so she'd know I was going to keep that secret.

"Well, goodnight," she said from the doorway as we angled forward into the wind. It was strong enough by then to force you backward if you didn't move deliberately.

Nordberg and I tried to talk a few times but it was pointless. The wind stole our words.

Chapter 15

When Harry Connelly came through his hotel room door, he saw me sitting in the darkness in a chair with my .44 aimed directly at his chest.

I'd gone there after I'd checked on Chuck Gage. He hadn't been home. I decided I'd make sure that Connelly understood that our deal was still on. He wouldn't kill Mike Chaney in exchange·for me not mailing a letter that didn't exist.

"Life is just full of surprises," he said, not wanting to give me the pleasure of seeing that he might be just a bit nervous. "My best friend sitting there pretending that he'd like to shoot me."

"I just wanted to check up on you and Pepper. Make sure you are still going to honor the deal we made."

"I need to get my prophylactics, Noah. You'll excuse me if I go over to my drawer. I hate the ones they have at the whorehouses. I always bring my own."

"Good for you. Now answer my question."

He went to the bureau, pulled out a cigar box, set it on the bureau top and opened the box. He held up two little packs. "The women, they really go for these, Noah."

"You use them when you and Pepper double up on a rape, do you?" They always liked to brag about those when the wine was down to dregs and the lamps to flickers.

He tucked the prophylactics into his coat pocket. "Noah, if I didn't know better, I'd think you had a low opinion of us."

He replaced the box in the drawer, the drawer in the bureau. "I'm meeting Mr. Pepper in just a few minutes."

"Remind him of our deal."

"You'll have to show me this famous letter of yours sometime, Noah. I must be getting as cynical as you are but I don't think I actually believe there is such a letter."

"There's only one way to find out."

He walked to the door. "Turn the covers back for me before you leave, Noah. I'll probably be too drunk to do it when I get back here tonight. We've all got an early start in the morning, don't we?" He adjusted his bowler. "We have to find the bad man, don't we?"

Chapter 16

Chuck Gage, the former mountain man who lived in a shed behind the Lutheran church, sounded groggy after I knocked. He came to the door saying "Jes' a danged minute, jes' a danged minute." He turned out to be a scruffy man in red long johns worn under a pair of dungarees held up by the widest suspenders I'd ever seen.

"Chuck Gage?"

"And who'd be askin'?"

"My name's Noah Ford. Jen Chaney told me you might help me with some questions about the mountains."

He shook his head.

"I should start chargin' you fellas."

"Which fellas would that be?"

"All you fellas want to go up into the mountains and find Chaney." Then: "I should invite you in. Do as much for you as I did for them."

Couple things right off about the comfortable one-room shack. The potbellied stove kept it nice and warm; the floor was wood and not packed earth; and the air smelled pleasantly of pipe tobacco, a scent I associate with my grandfather.

He had a comfortable-looking daybed with a handsome multicolored quilt for sleeping and two rocking chairs that looked handmade.

I stood facing him and said, "Man named Pepper come to see you?"

"Yeah. I didn't like him much."

"Not many people do."

"I had to help him because he was a federal man but I didn't help him much. I made sure I didn't." He flung his bony arm in the direction of a rocking chair. "Sit, sit."

I sat. "I got the impression from Jen that you might have told her brother where he could hide."

"And what would your interest be in this?"

"I'm a federal man, too. But I want to make sure that Chaney doesn't get killed."

"A federal man? Then you know them other two."

"Yeah."

"I don't trust 'em."

"Neither do I."

He lighted his corncob pipe with knobby hands.

The pipe tobacco scent reminded me of when my granddad would sit next to my bed and smoke his pipe and tell me bedtime stories. It's funny how you can revert to childhood so fast sometimes. My granddad had died a long time ago but I could remember the timbre and cadence of his voice. If there was a heaven, that would be the first sound I'd hear, the music of that old man's voice.

I said, "You know where Chaney is?"

"No. I've got a general idea. Told him I didn't

want to know exactly because then nobody could beat it out of me. But I have an idea of where he *probably* is. I spent most of my life up in them mountains. Be a blind fool if I didn't know where the best spots would be for hiding."

"I need to find him first."

He studied me long enough to make me uncomfortable.

"You ain't a bounty hunter on the side, are you? I've heard how federal boys file them reports. They catch the bad man then get some friend of theirs to claim that he caught the fella. The check goes to the friend and he splits it with the federal man."

"I'm not a bounty hunter."

"I didn't think so. Those fellas are always agitated. I used to be that way about pussy. I'd come down from the mountains three, four times a year and the minute I was around women—and I didn't care if they were ugly or pretty or skinny or fat or white or colored—I'd be so agitated I could barely control myself. But I always had to pay for pussy. No decent woman would want me. I could take five hot baths a day and I'd still smell like a mountain man. At least that's what all the decent women told me."

He sat back, rocked some more.

"But what these bounty boys is agitated about is money and the chance to kill somebody all legal-like. The money's nice, too, and they sure do want it. But what really works them up is hunting the man. So they get all worked up—it's just like havin' a hard-on and no woman around—and the only way they can get settled is to kill somebody. That's why they kill each other so often. Can't find nobody else and most lawmen don't give a damn about a bounty man getting killed. He probably figures 'good riddance.' " He paused. "But you ain't a bounty man so why you want him? And it ain't your case—leastways, Pepper said it was his and Connelly's—so what's your interest?"

"A friend of mine got killed tonight. The one everybody's blaming Mike Chaney for. But I don't think he did it."

"Who you after then?"

"Connelly and Pepper. That's where I'll start."

He grinned. "Then you're all right by me."

He set to rocking back and forth again. Smoking his pipe. The wind damned near knocked the shed over several times. God alone knew what held it up. He didn't seem to notice. He had his pipe and his stove and his rocking chair. He was almost serene.

"You ever meet Chaney?"

"Nope."

"I known him since he was a little boy. He was one of the nicest, kindest little boys I ever knew. And when he growed up, he was just the same way. And when he robbed banks, it was only Flannery banks because the Flannerys were dirty dealin' all the farmers and ranchers, not even givin' them any time at all to pay off their mortgages."

"Yeah, I know all that. Maybe he was right to do that, maybe he wasn't. My concern is that he's also a killer."

"That's the part that don't figure. He was the one who'd always step between and stop a fight, not start one. I seen him handle himself all right a couple times he had to. But killin' somebody—that just doesn't make any sense to me."

"Then I'm your best bet, Mr. Gage. You give me a map showing me where you think I'll find him—just the general area—and I promise you I'll do everything I can to bring him down that mountain alive."

He rocked some more. Stared straight at the stove door as if he could see images on it.

You had to be a little bit envious of Chaney. Having friends so loyal they'd hide him. Having friends so loyal they spoke of him as if he were not simply a legend but a saintly legend.

He yawned. "This is way past my sleepin' time."

"Sorry."

"When you figure on leaving?"

"Tomorrow morning."

He yawned.

"Stove gets me that sleepy. Never fails. Some nights I'm too lazy to even get up out of this old rocker. I just sleep in it all night."

"Wish I could sleep like that. Have a hard time with it a lot of nights. A lot of regrets, I guess."

For the first time, he laughed about something.

"I'm an innocent man, Mr. Ford. I ain't ever killed a man or made time with a married woman. I sleep like a baby." Then, and it was almost as if he was faking, his head lolled to the side and his eyes closed for a moment. He jerked back up out of his sudden sleep. "I'm too tired to do it now. You come back before you leave for the mountains in the morning. And I'll have a map all drawn for you and everything."

"I appreciate that very much."

"I'm fallin' asleep—"

And indeed he was.

Before I could even get to the door, the old man was snoring.

Chapter 17

Wind woke me only moments before the knocking. Dark door, dark window, cold floor as I tore my gun from the holster and said, "Who is it?"

"Jen."

What the hell time was it? What the hell was *she* doing there? Was there any possibility that this was a dream?

"Hurry up," she said.

I thought of something pretty damned ungentlemanly to say but I obeyed her siren call, anyway.

You could easily mistake her for a bear what with the parka and bulky butternuts she wore with a layer or two of long johns underneath.

She came in, shut the door. "Get the lamp lit. We need to hurry."

"What the hell's going on? What time is it, anyway?"

"What the hell's going on is that Connelly and Pepper left about ten o'clock last night for the mountains. And the time is four o'clock."

She didn't wait for me to turn up the lamp. She did

it herself. Meanwhile, I went to the window. The snow was churning pretty thick and already hinting at the fury to come.

"I'm just worried about their head start. I wasn't sleeping very much, anyway, worrying about Mike. So I got up to put on some coffee and then just decided to come and get you before it got real bad. Then the livery man—he sleeps right on the premises, the colored man does—told me that Connelly and Pepper had left about ten last night. And while I was there, I got you a horse."

"Do I get to go down the hall and wash up a little?"

"If you hurry."

"Yes, Commander."

"He's my brother."

"I know that, Jen. It's just that I'm never the happy sort in the morning, especially not when it's four in the morning."

"I'll try and remember that."

Any other time I might have taken that as a romantic clue. Standing there in long johns, cold feet and a full bladder, I knew better.

"Five minutes is about all we can spare, Noah. We really need to get going."

I forced myself to remember she was in a panic about her brother. I took ten minutes. She didn't look happy.

Soon as we were mounted up, both my saddlebags bloated with various things she thought I'd need for the trek, I told her about Chuck Gage.

"He said he'd draw me a map. But he wanted to get some sleep first."

She had to shout at me, the wind was so wild. "We'll have to wake him up."

At that rate, we'd have the whole town awake by four-thirty.

We ground-tied our horses and walked up to Chuck Gage's place. Smoke in the chimney was the only sign that anybody was inside.

Jen knocked.

"He sleeps a lot. I think all those years in the mountains finally took their toll. You can only have so many run-ins with death before you just start to fold up. Mike and I have an uncle like that. He was an old man before he was thirty-five."

She glanced at the door, then knocked again.

"I hope he worked up that map for us."

"Knock a little louder this time."

"Now who's giving the orders?"

"He might not hear us in this wind."

"For around here, this isn't much of a wind at all."

This time, she knocked with her fist, clublike, instead of just her knuckles. The door swung inward.

"Chuck? Chuck, are you in there?"

She didn't wait for an answer.

"I wonder if he's all right," she said, as she heaved the door inside.

No moon, no lamp. She held the door open as I came in and we both let our eyes adjust to the gloom.

Because the place was so small, it was easy to see what had happened in a single glance.

Chuck lay face down on the floor. One of the rocking chairs had been knocked over and several magazines had been scattered from on top of a small pine stand.

Jen was already kneeling next to him.

"He's alive." Then: "Chuck, it's Jen. We're going to help you sit up. Do you understand what I'm saying?"

His only response was a muffled moan. I got on the other side of him. We lifted him as gently as we could to his feet. His knees gave out with the slightest pressure on them. I got my arm under his and around his back. Jen did the same. We half-dragged him to the daybed.

We laid him on his back. She brought a jar of water and a white cloth over. We started looking for the spot on his head where he'd been hit. Easy enough to find, really. He'd been struck with something edged and hard—probably the handle of a handgun—just behind the ear. In his condition, it was easy enough to knock him out.

Jen soaked the rag and started to clean the wound. His eyes were still closed. He moaned every few seconds. Once, I was pretty sure he started to speak words. But the words were never finished. He went back to moaning.

I walked around the place. I could see melted snow tracked in by somebody's boots. The visitor had been there quite recently.

On the small table next to the two stacked orange crates he used as cupboards for his canned goods, I saw a paper where somebody—likely Chuck—had started to sketch out two maps.

I held them up for inspection. They were basically the same drawing but he had so many lines and erasures on the pages that it was hard to tell exactly what the map showed. No words identified the various points.

"What happened, Chuck?"

When I turned around to look at him, he was sitting up. Jen was still daubing at his wound.

"They just come in. Didn't knock or nothing. Come in and one of 'em grabbed me around the neck and got at me so he could strangle me. They didn't even say nothin'. They waited until I was choking before they even spoke to me." He started coughing. It went on for some time. She patted him on the back the way she would a baby. He kept staring at me. When he quit coughing, he said, "That's what I needed. A .44 like our friend has. I woulda cut 'em both down."

"Who were they, Chuck?"

He tried to talk but the coughing had cut in.

"Pepper and Connelly. They said they followed you here and wanted me to tell them what you and me talked about." More coughing. "Damned lungs. I don't think they quite healed up from the last time I had pneumonia. I just treated it myself. Maybe I shoulda gone to my doc."

"Your head still hurt, Chuck?"

"Yeah, but I'll get over it."

He looked at Jen. "You're a saint, Jen, you know that?"

"I'm not sure Mr. Ford there believes that."

"Aw, what's he know?"

Jen put her hands on his arms and began the slow process of laying him back down.

"Guess my head does still hurt a good piece."

"Of course it does. Now you just relax and lie still there."

"I had the map all set out for you when they came in. Did you see it over there on the little table?"

"It was gone. How long were you out, you think?" I asked.

"I was in and out, Noah. I'd try and get up and then I'd just fall back to sleep. I was real shaky. I thought I was gonna die. It was like a nightmare. My heart would be racin' and then my head would be poundin' and I'd hear the wind—"

Jen glanced at me and shook her head. No more questions for Chuck. And she was right. The assault had scared him. He was responding more to his fear of death than he was his actual pain. An old man, alone, a couple thugs like Connelly and Pepper knocking him out—death probably hadn't been far away and the terror of it still lingered in his eyes and shaky voice.

But there was one question I had to ask.

"Chuck, you think you could give Jen a good idea of where Mike might be?"

Given all his fear and pain, the smile was a surprise.

"Probably won't take long, Noah." To Jen, he said: "You remember a place called 'the dungeon'?"

"Sure. We used to play in it all the time." Now she smiled. "Sure. That would be the perfect place." To me: "It's a cave within a cave. Our folks forbid us to play in it but of course we did. It looks like just a small cave but if you wiggle your way through this opening in the back of it, there's this other cave that's probably a good twenty feet deep. Mike always said it reminded him of a dungeon. So that's what we called it."

"He's there. That's what I figure, anyway. I would've said that they'd never have found him but now that they have the map, they won't have any trouble except for the storm. But even then, that cave is only about a tenth of a mile off the main path up the mountain. If Mike has been outside and left any tracks—they could find him pretty easy."

The storm was the only thing I'd been worried about until we found Chuck. Now we had the storm and two killers to be concerned with. And it was hard to say which would prove more dangerous.

For the next ten minutes, Jen played nurse. She got Chuck settled onto his bed. She took the remains of the coffee, poured it into a tin cup, and set it on top of the potbellied stove to get reheated fast.

All I could think about was getting on that mountain path. I was sure they'd killed Daly and they'd damned near done in Chuck.

But Jen was now a mother of sorts and any man who tries to stop a mother from tending to one of her own is in big trouble.

"You ride into town and see the doc if your head gets any worse. You hear me, Chuck?"

"I hear ya, Jen."

"And don't go sampling any whiskey. You need to stay sober in case you *do* have to go see the doc."

He winked at me.

"She'd make a nice warden, wouldn't she?"

"You men wouldn't last a day without women to tell you what to do."

"Them mountain men seemed to do OK for themselves without women, Jen."

"That was only because they were part bear. I'm talking about normal men like you and Ford here. You just hate to admit that women know a lot more than you give them credit for."

"She also thinks women should get to vote, Noah."

"She sounds pretty radical to me, Chuck." Actually, I'd been in and out of Washington long enough to know that women, sooner than later, would be getting the vote. Then, I said: "We need to move, Jen. They've got a good head start on us."

So we said our goodbyes and went outside.

"You think he'll be all right?" Jen asked.

"It's not him I'm worried about. It's us. Connelly and Pepper have to know that we're not that far behind them. They'll probably try and bushwhack us."

"You sure have some nice friends, Ford."

We mounted up and started out of the yard. The foothills were maybe a quarter mile away, the mountain base a mile or so. Visibility kept getting worse because of the swirling dark clouds that were an ominous predictor of what was to come.

We were riding now for the last time. As soon as we reached the mountain upslope, we'd be walking our horses. The angle would be such that it was the only way to proceed safely.

As we neared the foothills, the acid in my stomach

started clawing at all the soft tissue in my gut, raising hell with it. I'd gone through the whole war like that. My stomach insisted on telling my brain what it didn't want to hear. That soon there would be trouble. Maybe real bad trouble.

PART TWO

Chapter 18

Didn't take me long to realize that it was going to be a journey of fits and starts. Wind and snow would whoop up on the narrow mountain trail we were ascending and I'd have to argue with Jen to give our horses a rest from fighting the headwinds and blinding snow.

Then we reached a natural cove made out of scrub pines. There wasn't any use trying to talk in that wind, so I turned in the saddle and pointed to the covelike formation of pines.

She didn't like it. She'd argued against the first time I'd told her we needed to stop. I understood her reason for wanting to keep going. I probably would have been just as single-minded if my brother was in the danger hers was.

She relented and we both dropped off our horses and led them to the area I'd pointed to. The temperature hadn't frozen my extremities yet. The wool scarf I had wrapped around my face had kept my nose and cheeks from freezing. But as I had to remind myself, we weren't even a fourth of the way toward reaching the mountain plateau where Chuck Gage had said Chaney was likely hiding.

The animals were white with snow. We brushed them off, though realistically in a few minutes they'd be white again.

"I'm not waiting more than fifteen minutes," she barked at me when we huddled inside the windbreak of the pines.

"I know you're in a hurry but there's something you're forgetting."

She laughed bitterly. "Let's make an agreement, all right? You don't know one damned thing about these mountains. I grew up here. So let's agree right now that you don't give me any more of your so-called advice, all right?"

"I may not know the mountains but I know horses." The snowstorm had put me in as bad a mood as it had her. "And I'll tell you one thing. One little piece of bad luck with our horses and then we'll really be behind Connelly and Pepper. There're a hundred places on this trail where our horses could stumble and hurt themselves. And then what? Then we're on foot."

But she was relentless. Her cold red cheeks and the snow trapped in her eyelashes had given her a doll-like look. But the dark eyes were angrier than ever. She might look like a doll but she was a damned angry one. "You think I haven't thought about the horses? But my brother's life is at stake here, federal man. This is just a job to you. But to me it's saving my own flesh and blood. So I'm going to push my horse as hard as I can. And if it breaks a leg and has to be shot, so be it. And if you don't like the way I'm pushing my horse, you can always head back. You want revenge for your friend. But your friend's already dead. My brother is still alive—at least hopefully. And I'm going after him right now whether you're with me or not. Now do you understand me, you stupid bastard?"

And with that, she stalked over to her horse and threw herself up on the saddle and headed back for the trail again.

We didn't speak for a good hour or more.

The snow thinned, the wind backed down some. The sun came out for ten minutes. It had a hallucinatory quality. Middle of a snowstorm—even if it had abated to a degree, it was still a snowstorm—you don't expect to see the sun. It put me in mind of all those desert stories where the man dying of thirst begins to imagine fountains and creeks. Was I imagining the sun?

"Maybe we're catching a break," she said.

I'd been expecting her to still be of the snarly persuasion. I didn't know if she always had this fierce side or if her brother's situation had created it. But now her voice was gentle, friendly.

"Is that really the sun?"

She laughed. "That's what I was thinking. I know people imagine they see things when they get snowblinded. But since we both see it maybe there's a possibility that it's really there."

I looked up to check on it again. A round golden ball throwing off waves of energy behind a screen of snow.

"I want to say something, Noah."

"You don't need to. I know you're sorry you snapped at me back there."

And she snapped at me again. "I was going to say that I was serious about you going back. I can do this alone."

"Oh."

"You really thought I was going to apologize?"

"Well, I thought it might at least be a possibility."

"Well, it isn't."

That didn't leave me with a whole hell of a lot to say. We plunged ahead.

About half an hour later, the snow still thin but the sun long gone, I heard Jen shout—heard the sound but not the word.

What I saw was Jen half-throwing herself off her horse. She landed on an icy patch just off the trail and skidded a couple feet before she was able to balance herself.

"She may have hurt herself," Jen said.

The horse held its foreleg daintily off the ground. It snorted softly.

I went over to it and brushed its face free of snow and then squatted down next to it. Jen was beside me within seconds.

After checking the hoof, we both took turns gently examining the areas of the forearm, knee, fetlock joint, and the pastern. Those were the most likely places where injury would have been done.

"We hit an icy patch that startled her and she sort of reared and when she came down on her weight, she limped a little. I got off her as soon as I could."

I kept touching parts of her lower leg. I couldn't feel any broken bones or swollen patches. But then bruises or muscle pulls could be just as painful.

Jen said: "I'm sorry for the way I've been acting. I always thought I did pretty well under pressure. But I'm finding out otherwise. I really am sorry."

"Like you say, he's your brother. I don't know that I'd be acting any better."

"Oh, sure. After all you've been through."

I stood up. Brushed my jeans off. "Before the war, this old sergeant told me that you never know who'll do well in battle. And he was right. Some of the really tough men just folded right up. And some of the quiet little men, who didn't look like very much, they kept calm and helped the other soldiers all through the war. And a situation like this is no better. You're holding up very well."

She leaned over and kissed me on the cheek. Then laughed. "Your cheek is like marble. Could you even feel my lips?"

"Not much. Maybe if we ever get in a nicer spot, we'll try that again."

She smiled and then looked down at her horse's leg. The foot was on the ground now.

"Think I should try and walk her?"

"Worth a try. Just take it slow."

She nodded, picked up the reins.

We both muttered curses when the animal took its first step. A decided limp.

She halted the animal. "I don't want to hurt her."

"Let's see if she can walk it off. If it's muscular, that's at least a possibility."

A wave of sprayed snow covered a wide area, including us. It had the feel of somebody sprinkling salt on you.

"All right," she said. "Guess I should try one more time."

You always feel sorry for the horse in a moment like that, but being a selfish human being, your own needs are stronger than your pity and so you watch with more objectivity than you should. The horse limped four more times when pressure was put on the damaged leg.

"I just can't put her through this anymore, Noah."

"Keep going."

"Are you sure?"

"Just keep going."

I'd been around enough military horses in enough military situations to know that sometimes the animals could surprise you—and probably themselves—if you kept pushing.

And that was what she did, finally.

Limp limp limp.

And Jen frowning and cooing and making maternal sounds.

And then—no limp.

Three, four, five times, no limp.

And this time, it wasn't just a peck on the cheek I got.

This time it was arms thrown around my neck and our lips lingering on each other for a good long time.

Chapter 19

Later in the afternoon, after the snow and wind had abated for nearly an hour, we picked up tracks their horses had left in a stretch of powdery snow. No wagon tracks, though. Anybody who lived in the foothills had probably stayed inside that day, fearing the snow.

Because there was no ice on that stretch, we made good time on the snow, leading our horses up the first slope. We'd already made our decision about that night. Jen talked about the cabin we could stay in if luck got us there before full night. We could travel in the dark, with or without moonlight, but the biggest part of the trip would be the next day and we would need a night's sleep for that.

Luck didn't hold.

Snow began to swirl again as the long shadows of early dusk began to stretch across the valley below us. The temperature was holding so we didn't have to worry about frostbite but the cabin she'd talked about sounded a lot better than a jury-rigged lean-to.

My horse began to tire. I held up my hand for us to halt.

I fed my horse, cleaned off the snow, and then led him into some pines so he could get out of the slowly increasing wind for a while.

"How far you think this cabin of yours is?"

She smiled. "You sound like you don't believe me."

"I guess I was under the impression that it was closer by than it is."

"An hour or two at most, if the snow holds off and the wind doesn't get mean." She put out her mittened hand. "Would you say a prayer with me? For Mike?"

"You'll have to say it. I haven't been in a church for a long time."

"You never pray?"

I shrugged. "Sometimes, late at night, I suppose. But it's not exactly praying. I just try to figure things out more than anything."

"Figure what things out?"

"I'm not sure you'd want to hear it."

"The war?"

I hesitated. "Yeah."

"My Uncle Don is like that. My aunt says he still wakes up in the middle of the night. Sometimes he screams and sometimes he gets violent. Gets up and starts smashing things. But when she calms him down he doesn't have any memory of it."

"I think you can see too much death and it changes you and you can never be right again."

She took my hand. "I'm sorry, Noah." Then: "You ready?"

"Let's give it a try."

She said a prayer and she sounded like a little girl

standing on that slope with dusk revealing the stars that had been hiding there all along, bright and perfect and so above the misery below. She was sweeter in that moment than anybody had been to me in a long, long time. And afterward she slid her arm around me and we just held each other as wolves began to cry somewhere deep in the timber.

There are Indian shamans who believe that you can tell a place where great evil has recently occurred. They say that they can see a glow around the top of the site. I've been told this by two or three shamans of very different tribes. Each time it was told to me in great earnestness.

I thought of this when I stood on the hill overlooking the cabin in a small bowl-like valley beneath us. We'd worked our way up two long steep slopes, one of which was perilously close to the edge of the trail. Far below us, we could see a tiny cabin flanked by a stretch of pine trees.

I took out my field glasses and looked the cabin over. For some reason, I remembered what those shamans had told me. About evil having a hue in the form of a halo effect.

I didn't see any glow but I did see a couple of things that simple deduction told me were way wrong.

Two horses lay dead on their sides in front of the cabin. A wagon had been turned over. The storm had been bad in patches but not bad enough to kill horses or pitch wagons upside down.

Before we started down the long slope leading to the flat below, I pulled my repeater from its scabbard.

"Any particular reason for a rifle?" Jen asked.

I told her what I'd seen. "I'd say we don't need any more trouble but we have to rest the horses and sleeping in a cabin sounds mighty nice right now."

She nodded to the metal of my rifle barrel, gleaming in the moonlight. "I take it you expect trouble."

"Not expect, necessarily. But worry about. Something went pretty wrong down there." I shrugged. "But maybe we'll be surprised. Maybe the horses ate bad food. Maybe that wagon's been overturned for a long time."

"You really believe that?"

"Probably not."

The trek down wasn't easy. We walked our horses. The snow was deep and dangerous, had probably accumulated over the previous two or three mountain snows.

Jen fell face first into the snow and I helped dig her out; and a few minutes later she returned the favor.

I kept looking for some kind of ambush. Tired travelers seeing the cabin, disregarding the dead horses and the overturned wagon, decided to work their way down and see what had happened. And maybe get a snug resting place for the night, after all.

And run right into the gun sights of road agents. That was the kind of lure a lot of them favored.

"I'm starting to get a bad feeling about that cabin down there, Noah."

"Me, too."

"I don't want to turn back but I think we need to be ready to shoot."

I nodded.

A clear night then, even the cold tolerable, we should have been happy to find the cabin. But we both knew better.

The first horse lay a hundred yards east of the cabin. I left my own horse and went to have a look at it. I found what I expected to find. The animal had been shot twice in the head from a fair distance.

The other horse lay closer to the cabin. It had died the same way. In the moon glow its rigid form, including the frozen red blood on its neck and head, had an ugly beauty to it. Even the splattered shit, splattered on dying, was somewhat redeemed by the snow. Something you'd see in a painting meant to shock.

Jen stood quietly by, her expression shifting from anger at the death she saw, to eyes closed in a prayer said silently.

Then we stood together, facing the cabin; the dark and quiet cabin, a crudely built arrangement of logs and finished lumber. No windows. No smoke from the chimney. No sound but our own horses snorting and fretting while they stood ground-tied behind us. They were responding to the deaths of their own kind. Even though the dead animals were snow-covered and the blood hardened, our horses were aware of them and were spooked.

My voice was startling in the enormous silence: "If anybody's in there, come out with your hands up. My name is Noah Ford and I'm a federal agent. I just want to know what happened here."

The slight wind provoked ghost dances of frolicking snow, merry mountain ghosts who disdained any knowledge of the carnage there—and the carnage I expected to find inside.

"Maybe they're afraid to come out," Jen said.

"Maybe."

"Or maybe nobody's in there."

"Maybe."

"You get real quiet when you work."

"Uh-huh." Then: "I've got a railroad watch here and when I see a minute's gone by I'm going to start emptying my rifle into the door there. You can make this a lot easier for everybody if you just come out."

"You really going to fire into that door?"

"We'll see, I guess."

I hadn't pulled my watch out. I had no idea how long a minute was. I'd just fake it.

"We don't even know who's in there. Maybe somebody completely innocent."

"Look. Maybe somebody's in there who saw Connelly and Pepper and can tell us something about them. I've already given them warning inside. If they're so innocent, why didn't they answer?"

"Maybe they're wounded."

"I'm going to put the bullet high into the door."

"It could still hit somebody."

I got mad and didn't try to hide it. "You're so worried about your brother, why are you so worried about who's inside?"

"There's just no sense in hurting somebody who didn't have anything to do with taking Mike."

I was sick of arguing. I put the bullet where I said I would. The echo was enormous. Wolves cried again.

We stood in the snow, waiting.

I cupped my hands around my mouth. "The next time I'm going to put a lot more bullets into that door. And I'm bound to hit you sooner or later. So come out now, just like I told you."

At first, I couldn't figure out what the answering response was. A large bird of some kind? A wounded animal?

"It's a child, Noah."

"You sure?"

"I've probably been around a lot more kids than you have."

A wind whooped up. Sparkling spirals of snow danced around us again.

"Could be a trap. Somebody just pretending to be a kid."

"Lord, Noah, it's a kid, all right? I know a kid when I hear one."

"Then I need to go up to the door."

"I'll go with you."

"No. You stay here with your carbine. I'm going to work off the side of the door. Roll in front of it and kick it in as I'm rolling past. You be ready to shoot whoever appears in the doorway. If they're carrying a gun."

The sound came again.

A child was crying. No doubt about it now.

"Let me go up there."

"Jen, we know there's a kid in there. But that's all we know. Somebody else could be in there, too. And a kid could always kill you, too."

"I'll go. You cover me instead."

That probably wasn't a tale I'd tell later on. The night I stood by and let a woman do my job for me.

Yep, didn't have any idea who was in that cabin but I let the gal go in. Why get my own ass shot up? Just send the gal in there.

You don't hear talk like that in a dime novel. If you did, the readership would go way, way down.

"I can't let you do that."

"Sure you can. You're better with a gun. But this is a child and I'm better at talking to her. Or him. A woman's voice is a lot more soothing than a man's."

She was probably right.

"So cover me, all right?"

"Yes, boss."

"Don't worry, Noah. I won't ever tell anybody about it. I know how it'd look to that big strong male club you belong to."

She hefted her carbine, tugged up her mittens, and then set off for the cabin. The kid had made no other sound.

I sighted my rifle.

Jen didn't do any of the gymnastics I'd had in mind. She just trudged up to the door, stood to the side of it and knocked.

"I want to help you, honey. Why don't you come out? I have a friend who doesn't trust people very much so maybe you should put your hands in the air, too, so he can see that you aren't planning on shooting anybody. He can't help it. It's just the way he thinks. Now come on out, honey. We want to help you."

Two, three silent minutes passed. The door stayed shut. Jen looked back at me a couple of times. I couldn't read her expression from where I stood.

"Honey, please make things easy for all of us. Just please come out here and have your hands in the air. Then we'll talk and my friend won't have to shoot anymore."

This time, it wasn't just crying. The child was sobbing.

"Honey, can you hear me?" she asked.

Faint—a different sound. A word I couldn't understand.

Then: "Y-yes, I can hear you."

"I want to help you."

"I'm scared now."

These words I heard only because I had moved closer.

"Will you open the door and let me in?"

"What's your name?"

"Jen. That's short for Jenny. Do you know anybody named Jenny?"

Long pause. "Back in Illinois I did."

"Is that where you're from?"

"Yes."

"We could talk better if you would open the door, honey."

"My mommy said I shouldn't open the door for anybody."

"Where's your mommy now?"

"On the floor."

"Is she asleep?"

"The man hurt her. He made her get naked. She told me not to watch. He made her get naked and then he did things to her. And then he started hitting her real hard."

Jen hung her head after the girl spoke. Not easy hearing a little girl describe the apparent rape and beating of her mother. But Jen recovered quickly. She showed me a face of such murderous anger that I knew my impression of her was right. This wasn't a woman who let go easily. This was a woman who would hunt you down.

"Please open the door, honey. I'm with a lawman and we both want to help you."

"Are you a lawman, too?"

"No, but I'm with a lawman."

"She's helping me," I said. "So it's safe to let both of us in."

The easiest way to get in was to kick the door in. Didn't look like it would take all that much. But the girl needed to trust us and kicking in the door wasn't going to help things.

"You won't hurt me?"

"No," Jen said. "We want to help you. What's your name?"

"Clarice."

"That's a beautiful name. Now, Clarice, why don't you open the door so we can help you and your mommy?"

"You promise you won't hurt me?"

"We promise, Clarice," I said.

After a long silence from inside, the door latch was raised and the door moved slowly inward.

A skinny blond girl, couldn't have been more than

seven or eight years old, in pigtails and dungarees and a heavy red sweater stood in the doorway. Her hands were an even darker red—blood red—than her sweater.

As soon as I reached the doorframe, I smelled it. Butchered meat. Human, animal. The stench is similar.

Jen reached in and put her arms out to Clarice. Clarice came to her. Jen lifted her up, hugged her, carried her out into the night. "Maybe some fresh air will help." She looked at me when she said it. I didn't need to ask what she was talking about.

The only interior light was spill from the moon. The odor was so bad I had to hold my breath for a time.

I found a lantern. Took a stick match from my pocket. Got it fired and got the lantern glowing.

I didn't go to the woman right away because I'd stumbled against something at my feet.

He'd been wearing a heavy red sweater like his sister's, dungarees, heavy winter boots that laced up to near his knees. His right hand clutched a bowie knife. There was no blood on the blade. He was a towhead like his sister, two years older or so. There was no help for him. His wide-open eyes stared up at the roof of the cabin. Clarice must have felt the loss of her mother to the degree that she'd forgotten her brother entirely. Or maybe she couldn't own up to what had happened to him.

I looked around the place. Table, two chairs, a second table that had probably held the canned goods strewn across the floor, a small potbellied stove—just about all of it was demolished, a couple of the cans so dented that they'd exploded. There had been some frantic and furious activity in there.

Two whiskey bottles had been smashed. The contents of a carpetbag had been dumped on the floor. And then I saw the broom.

At first I wasn't sure what to make of it. A straw broom with an unpainted pine handle. The end of the handle was bloody. I moved closer to it and saw small curly pieces of black hair and then splotches of what seemed to be human tissue. And then I realized what I was looking at.

I went over, took a deep breath, and finally took a look at the woman. They say some Indians will do things to a white woman that they wouldn't do to an animal. That's what this looked like except there hadn't been any Indians involved. Just a pair of white men who had their badges to protect them.

Clarice had covered her with a heavy woolen blanket the color of a summer-green leaf. Blood had soaked much of it.

They had cut off her nose, pounded her right eye into a bruised and enormous lump, and then gone to work on her body. Bite marks alternated with knife slashes. Her right nipple was gone, the crudeness of the wound suggesting that it had been bitten off.

When I saw her genitals the picture of the broom handle came to me. Both of them taking turns with her and then killing her with the broom handle, the little boy trying to free his mother by stabbing them and getting himself killed in the process.

I couldn't explain how Clarice had survived. There were no good places for hiding in this cabin. Maybe she had escaped somehow and they'd figured she wasn't worth the trouble of tracking down. Even by their standards, this was grotesque.

From outdoors, I could hear the soft crunching sounds of Jen's feet in the snow. And Jen cooing to Clarice as she carried her around the way she would a baby. Treating the little girl the way she would treat a skittish fawn. Slowly, gently, speaking words that were almost cooing sounds.

I needed to get out of the cabin if only for a few minutes. Jen by then had Clarice on her lap—sitting on a box she'd found in the overturned wagon apparently—rocking her back and forth, letting the girl cry.

I didn't bother them. I rolled myself a smoke and walked a ways upslope. I'd thought the clean air would help but it didn't. I walked downwind of the cabin, so they wouldn't be able to see what I'd done, and vomited on the far side of a copse of small pines. That helped. I hadn't smoked the cigarette I'd made. The puking had been too urgent.

I reached down and scooped up a handful of snow and stuffed it into my mouth. After I spit it out, the worst of the vomit taste was gone. Then I smoked the cigarette.

I wondered how much whiskey they'd brought with them. They'd be good for anything if they had enough whiskey. I knew then that it was damned unlikely Mike Chaney would be brought back to town alive.

Being in the cabin had drained me. I needed at least a few hours' sleep and I was sure Jen did, too.

Jen had taken a blanket from her horse and swaddled Clarice in it. Then she'd propped Clarice up against the overturned wagon. The girl appeared to be fast asleep.

"I've got just enough energy to cut down some of those pine branches and build us a lean-to. Then we can get started early morning."

"The trees are close enough. I can hear her if she cries or something. Let me help you."

I needed to smile. "You're going to get me kicked out of that he-man's club yet."

"Oh, I have a feeling they'd never kick you out. You've got a streak of mean in you that'll get you through about anything."

Then I didn't feel like smiling at all. A streak of mean.

We cut the branches together but putting the lean-to together fell to me.

Jen came over. She was as pale as the snow.

She held Clarice in her arms.

"We'll have to take her with us," I said.

"Good. I was afraid you'd say we'd have to turn back."

"He's your brother but I want those two bastards even more than you do right now."

"Clarice described them to me a while ago. One of them is definitely Connelly. Him I saw around town. I never actually saw the other one. Pepper."

"The mother and boy we'll have to leave here for the time being."

"There'll be animals."

"There's a lot of firewood in the back. I'll carry it

around here and stack it up in front of the door. No windows for them to crawl through."

"She'll keep asking me about her mother and brother. She won't want to leave."

I started rolling another cigarette. Then: "You looked inside?"

She nodded.

"You saw the broom?"

"Yeah. I didn't have guts enough to pull the cover back and look at the mother, though."

I knew it was time to get busy. "I'll start stacking the firewood in front of the door now."

"You sure work hard."

"Keeps my mind busy so I don't have to remember what I saw in the cabin."

"I wonder if Clarice'll be able to forget?"

"She mention her brother?"

"Just once. I saw him when I looked in through the door. He was trying to protect his mother."

"You go to the lean-to. I'll stack the firewood."

I went over and started on the wood. Physical labor felt good. It would make me sleep instead of just being fatigued. A good hard three hours of blackness would give me back my strength.

Work up a sweat and give in to just becoming a mule. There is something about that kind of labor that we all need from time to time. I worked out of the agency office for four months and finally tendered my resignation. A desk is not for me. They put me back on fieldwork.

When I finished blocking up the doorway to the cabin, I grabbed my saddle blanket from my horse and went to the lean-to. The wind wasn't so bad just then.

Clarice was on Jen's lap again, saying: "But won't my mommy get cold?"

"We'll put plenty of blankets on her, honey."

"Will she wake up to say goodbye?"

"We should just let her sleep, honey. We won't be gone that long and then we'll come back here and take both of you back to town."

I couldn't figure out any way to say it any better. Maybe the kid knew the truth even without us telling her. Maybe she knew the truth but didn't want us to say it. Maybe it was the only way she could deal with it—putting it off till she was stronger.

The wind stayed down most of the night. We ended up huddled together because the temperature dropped several degrees. We were awakened twice by Clarice's screams. Nightmares. They would curse her the rest of her life.

At dawn we discussed coffee. We both wanted it but building a fire would waste time. We ate jerky and bread and drank water from the canteens.

When we were getting the horses ready to move, Clarice got away from us and worked her way back toward the cabin. She hadn't seen the firewood I'd stacked in front of the door. In the light I saw what a poor defense it was. Any number of animals could rip it down and get inside.

But that wasn't what bothered Clarice. She stood in front of the cabin and started sobbing.

I got to her first and lifted her up. "What's wrong, honey?"

"That wood. How's my mommy ever going to get out of there?"

Then Jen was there. She took her and carried her away. I couldn't hear what they were saying but as the sun began to paint the snow hills a rich gold, Clarice stopped crying.

Getting upslope took a lot longer than getting downslope had. We didn't reach the mountain trail for a good hour. The horses were still tired and, much as we didn't want to admit it to each other, so were Jen and I.

Clarice rode Jen's horse. We walked. And after a while, so quietly that you could barely hear it in the growing wind, Clarice cried. Jen would call words to her but that was about all they seemed to be. Words. They didn't slow the little girl's crying at all.

And for the first time, magnanimous son of a bitch that I am, I felt resentment toward the little girl. She was slowing us down. And what if she kept up crying like this? And how could we confront Connelly and Pepper with a kid in tow? And what if she started bawling when we snuck up on them?

That little brat was all kinds of trouble.

And then finally I realized what a bastard I was being.

I needed sleep. I hadn't had a good bowel movement in three days. Tom Daly's wife was going to blame me for Tom's death.

The kid wasn't the trouble; my life was the trouble.

She'd had to watch her brother be murdered and her mother raped and murdered in just about the worst way you could think of. And she was only seven years old.

And here I was feeling sorry for myself because I hadn't had a good stool for seventy-two hours.

What a magnanimous bastard I am.

Chapter 20

That afternoon, the wind was the worst of it, strong enough to blow you back several steps so that a good share of your walking was covering what you'd already been over.

The mountain was a soaring wall that blocked out a good deal of sky. The very top was often lost in snow swirls that were like exotic mists in an adventure story. Even the wolves we saw looked whipped and beaten by the weather, hidden just a few feet off the path, their eyes lurid and lonely. Two or three times I smelled and heard bear but never actually saw one.

Clarice slept as she rode, bundled up mummy-like in blankets.

Always, relentless, there was the wind, the sounds it made in the mountain rocks above alternately friendly and eerie. Whenever I was in the mountains I always thought of how many different centuries of men had lived in them. The cries of the wind sometimes sounded like the cries of ghosts all the way back to when men hunted with clubs and sharpened stones and feared animals we couldn't even imagine now.

The wind blinded us, too. Visibility was at most ten, twelve feet, occasionally much less. The path was straight so that kept us on track, anyway.

Darkness came quickly.

Jen was eager to push forward but I said no. Another storm was on its way. The cloud mass and color told that. She argued that we could probably reach her brother's hiding place soon; two, three hours at most.

I didn't argue. I just tied down my horse and went looking for firewood. When I got back she'd set up a lean-to. Clarice sat bundled inside it, eating some of the bread and jerky Jen had given her. Jen didn't speak to me. I didn't blame her for worrying about her brother but I wasn't ready to die in a night of near-blizzard conditions.

The fire proved to be a bitch. Wind and snow assaulted not only us but set the forest areas to swaying so hard that you could hear timber crack. I did well enough to heat up coffee and beans but then the wind changed directions and put the fire out for good.

That night Jen and Clarice stayed on one side of the lean-to and I stayed on the other. She had answered a grand total of three of my questions since we'd made camp. One-word answers. She was many things, this Jen I felt closer and closer to all the time, but forgiving was not one of them. My apology might have helped the situation. But I didn't make a habit of apologizing when I felt I was in the right.

The storm that had stopped around midnight whipped up again just before dawn. It was of enough strength to make traveling impossible. It was wind and snow equally. This fortunately was brief though it had turned into sleet.

When the storm died we quickly set off.

Jen was familiar with what we needed to do to find the cave. She signaled where we turned east along a narrow trail through heavy timber.

She was speaking to me again. Not in the way she usually did. She was taking it slow, making me appreciate each modest advance. The previous night had been one word answers. We were up to two-word answers by then with the prospects of three-word answers on the horizon.

Clarice apparently had a nightmare about her mother. During an odd silence in the woods, she began screaming so hard she fell off the horse. The blankets she'd been wrapped in broke her fall. She wasn't hurt but she'd been stunned out of the lingering nightmare.

Amazing how maternal and tender Jen could be when she was still mostly ignoring me. She held the kid tight and rocked her back and forth and started saying those half-whispered words that sounded like cooing again.

The sun appeared midafternoon, just as we came to an outcrop of rock.

And that was when we met up with Connelly and Pepper.

They had left the outcropping so they could fire at us from the left, from up on a hill that gave them pine-heavy cover. Exposed like that, we were much easier targets.

We dismounted quickly, Jen grabbing Clarice. We managed to scramble behind a thin copse of pine.

They had to kill something to amuse themselves so they took our horses. At the sound of the gunfire the horses spooked and made the mistake of turning to the edge of the outcropping. My horse was shot twice in the face and pitched sideways off the trail. Jen's horse fell, too, but balanced perilously on the edge of the outcropping. Its legs jerked as it died, propelling her horse over the edge.

The trouble was the trees were sparse and from their perch on the hill, Connelly and Pepper could see us without much trouble.

I couldn't get any kind of clean shot off. I needed to get closer but in order to do that I'd have to move closer to the trail. This would invite a barrage of gunfire. Getting killed was part of my job. But neither Jen nor Clarice had signed on for that. I needed to get them to a place that was safer than that relatively open place.

The gunfire kept Clarice's crying at a constant keen, making even Jen sob every once in a while. They wanted to kill us but they wanted to have some fun doing it.

I lifted Jen's Colt from her holster.

I said, "I'm going to start returning fire. You take the kid and start running for the timber as soon as I do."

Jen didn't argue. She probably would have stayed and done her own shooting but it was the kid she was worried for.

My rifle was in the scabbard on my animal. All I had was my .44. But it would be enough to force them to take cover while Jen and Clarice made it to the woods.

"Now!" I shouted.

I started firing like crazy, emptying Jen's gun into the air in the general direction of their position. This got the response I'd hoped for. Just as I got into a crouching position, preparing to throw myself onto the trail and roll to the relatively safe haven of the forest where Jen and Clarice were about to hide—just then the air became furious with two men who had decided to give up playing and start firing in earnest. And they would start with me. And after I was dead, they'd have Jen to have some fun with. Maybe even the same kind of fun they'd had with Clarice's mother. Clarice screamed as Jen picked her up, tucked her under her arm, and started moving as fast as she could on the slick surface of snow.

But before I reached the trees where Jen and Clarice were hiding, I wanted to get my rifle. I would have to be damned quick—my horse was close by but right out in the open—but a repeater and ammunition were the only way we were going to survive.

I kept pumping bullets at the outcropping, even though they'd now retreated behind a tree at the edge of the rock they were firing from.

I stood up, keeping my head down to avoid them using it as a target. Ten years before I could have pulled that trick off without undue risk of getting a few fairly serious holes put in my skull.

But I wasn't that fast anymore and I'd be jumping from a very slippery surface, which could mean that my jump might not be clean. I'd be a good target for them but I wouldn't even have a chance at getting the rifle. But I didn't have any choice. I readied myself for my jump. Deep breath. Two deep breaths.

I stuffed my .44 in its holster. And then I jumped.

It took them a few seconds to see me. They didn't wait to think through what I was doing. They didn't need to. They saw me jump and then reach the dead animal and then rip the repeater from its scabbard.

In those seconds they fired a war's worth of rounds.

The jump worked fine. But as soon as I had the repeater in my hand, my boot heels skidded on the icy surface of the trail and I went over backward.

I didn't want to lose the rifle. It could easily slide away. So I clutched it as hard as I could and just gave in to the fall. I wasn't worried about going over the edge. But I sure didn't want to crack my head open, either.

I held my head up as I hit the ground. My shoulders took a lot of the impact. My hand still gripped the rifle.

I started rolling toward the edge of the woods. Bullets ripped up snow bursts all around me, coming closer and closer.

I was able to angle myself behind some bushes and lay there while they pumped shots endlessly near and around me.

I still had maybe six feet to go before I reached the woods proper. A clear six feet. I'd once again be a clear target.

I got up on my haunches. From there I could see Jen and Clarice behind a huge boulder just inside the line of woods.

Their firing let up. Reloading no doubt. And probably trying to give me a false sense of security.

Sure, I could make that six-foot run from that

wide, open spot on the trail. They wouldn't hurt me. They'd be too busy loading their rifles.

But I was wrong. One of them had apparently reloaded because three bullets sizzled past me. I ducked but in doing so I fell to my knees on the ice.

A rabbit on my right got my attention. It was trying to get enough traction to get moving again. The surface of the snow away from the outcropping was sufficiently slick to qualify as an ice-skating rink.

No way could I survive a direct run to the woods. Not with one of them still able to fire at me. But the rabbit gave me an idea. All I needed was for the surface of the snow to cooperate. If it was sufficiently frozen it would be able to support me and I'd skid right into the woods.

No time to debate. The move I made was similar to riding a sled. I needed to get some traction and then I needed to hit the ground in such a way that the icy surface would help me slide right across and into the woods. Hopefully I'd be moving fast enough— and giving them a big enough surprise—that their bullets wouldn't be able to find me in time.

I sent my rifle skidding across the ice to the edge of the woods. It would be too cumbersome to keep with me.

Then I decided to jackpot. Either I'd soon be relatively safe or I'd be seriously wounded or maybe even dead.

I slammed my body down as I had when I spent long winter afternoons sledding as a kid.

Then I was off the trail and sliding along the surface of the snow. Jen was screaming for me to hurry up! Hurry up! She didn't seem to understand that I was skidding as fast as I could.

Another round of gunfire from Connelly and Pepper. Stench of gunfire; crack of bullets smashing into branches and ice-covered snow.

Jen dragged me into the woods the way she would have dragged a drowning man across a beach.

I got to my feet, brushed myself off.

Clarice stood next to Jen. She looked alert in a way I hadn't seen before.

"Are they the men who killed my mommy?"

She said it simply, almost without emotion.

Jen glanced at me then leaned over close to Clarice and said, "Yes, honey. Those are the men."

"Will they be hanged?"

"Yes, honey, they will."

She turned her small face to me.

"Will you hang them?"

"No, but I'll arrest them and see that they get hanged." I spoke in ragged, broken bursts. I had no breath left and my body was half-frozen from sweat.

I leaned down and gave Clarice a kiss on the head.

Maybe someday we'd know why she had suddenly realized—or allowed herself to realize—that her mother and brother were dead.

Jen said, "I have a box of bullets for your carbine. I brought one from home. So we still have that, anyway."

"How far is it to your brother's cave?"

"No more than half an hour."

"I wonder why Connelly and Pepper were waiting for us instead of being at the cave."

"Mike has the advantage. In order to shoot him, they have to lean over the top of the cave to see where they're shooting. He could pick them off."

"But if they put enough bullets down there—"

"Yeah. Enough bullets and the way bullets will ricochet off the walls—they'd hit him eventually. The cave isn't that big. And even if he gets to the hidden cave they can wait him out." Bitter smile. "They never did mean to bring him in alive, did they?"

"I thought I had a deal with them. But then when Mike got accused of killing Tom Daly—"

"I just keep thinking of what they did back at the cabin to Clarice's mother and brother—" Then she stopped herself. Her eyes got a sheen on them and I thought she was going to cry. But she made an obvious effort not to and said, "Let's get going."

She knew a path through the woods. No evidence of fresh footsteps. There was a good chance we'd be safe taking that route. Connelly and Pepper would be looking for us on the mountain trail.

The afternoon had turned mild enough for us to catch glimpses of forest animals watching us move along. Fascinating creatures, human beings, me being one and all. But for the most part, I still preferred the company of so-called dumb animals.

We tried to make as little noise as possible, but feet on icy snow aren't exactly quiet. I led and every few minutes or so I'd stop to listen for any extra sounds the wind might be carrying. Connelly and Pepper wouldn't be much better in this kind of terrain than I was.

We all needed toilet stops at different times. I'd just finished mine, washing my hands in the snow and setting off to the path again, when a voice from above said, "Stop right there. I've got a carbine trained right on the back of your neck."

I assumed it was Connelly or Pepper. But when the voice spoke again I realized it was too young and clear—no tobacco, no whiskey in that voice—to be either one of them.

"Get my sister back here."

I took my hat off and stared up, trying to find a face among the snow-heavy branches of the scrub pine. I got a glimpse of one but that was all.

"You Mike?"

"That's right. I saw your badge so I don't have to ask who *you* are."

"I've told your sister that I'd give you every chance to tell your story." My neck was getting a crick from having to look straight up.

I didn't have to go get Jen and Clarice after all. They ran down the path toward me.

"Who're you talking to?"

"Your brother."

Mike said, "I knew you'd remember the cave, Jen. But I had to leave there. I was out hunting some meat and when I came back I saw them outside the cave. With rifles. So I couldn't get back to my horse. I'm on foot now. They sure didn't look like the kind who'd bring me in alive. I figured them for bounty men."

"Yes, that's exactly what they are. Gosh, I wish you were down here so I could give you a hug."

"That's some baggage you're carrying, Jen. A lawman and a little girl. What's the story?"

"This is Clarice, Mike. We found her back at that

old cabin. We couldn't leave her there, so we brought her with us."

Mike didn't say anything, but the fact that she'd brought Clarice along, there, looking for him, told him something about the situation back at the cabin.

Jen pointed at me. "And this is Noah Ford. He's a good man, Mike. He wants to hear what you have to say. And then bring you back to town peacefully. He used to work with the two men you saw. They're federal agents but they're also killers."

"And he isn't, I suppose?"

"He's trying to help, Mike."

"That what this man is? Federal?"

I said, "That's what I am, Mike. But why don't you come down here?"

"Then lean your rifle against the tree behind you. And hand your .44 to Jen."

No reason not to, I thought. So that was what I did. He came down monkey-swift, monkey-sure, dropping from a heavy branch when he had a clear path.

They were brother and sister, all right. Pioneer stock, hard work keeping them trim, intelligent faces. He wore a green sweater and a green hunting cap, green being a good color when you wanted to fade into the forest.

They hugged. They hugged so long that Clarice looked up at me and actually smiled. And then she made a winsome face and gave me a shrug of her shoulders. She seemed to be amused by all the hugging. But soon enough her face was dour again, the gaze frightened.

When they finished hugging, Jen slid her arm

around his waist and laid her head on his shoulder. She explained who Clarice was and what had happened in the cabin.

"They sound pretty dangerous, Ford. You going to turn me over to them?"

"No."

"You want to put cuffs on me?" Mike asked.

"Not if you won't cut and run."

"I didn't kill anybody, Ford. I honest-to-God didn't."

"Well, when we get back to town, we'll sit down and talk about it. Right now while we've got some decent weather, let's make as much time as we can." To Jen, I said, "When Clarice gets too tired to walk, I'll carry her."

"You think I can't carry her?"

Mike laughed.

"Never tell my sister she isn't strong enough to do something. She'll prove you wrong."

We'd been four hours walking. I suggested we rest up before we start the trek back. Jen looked relieved. Clarice said, "You have any more licorice, Jen?"

Jen smiled, reached in her pocket, and gave her a six-inch black twist of the stuff.

Mike and I tore down pine branches and made a place for everybody to sit down.

When we were all sitting under the shelter of a huge pine, Jen put Clarice on her lap and began rocking her. In very little time, they both appeared to be asleep.

I said, "Somebody in town wants you dead. Connelly and Pepper didn't kill the federal man and for some reason I'm not sure they killed Tom Daly."

"That's why I ran, Ford. Like you said, somebody in town's got it in for me. Most people are grateful that I robbed Flannery's banks. But you live in a town as long as Sis and me have, you naturally get enemies."

"Especially when you steal from the richest man around, to say nothing about chasing women the way you do."

He shrugged. "Flannery's got it coming. You know that. And as for the women, well let's just say it wasn't always me chasing them. Sometimes it was them chasin' me. And I don't mean to be braggin'. I just mean—well, I did some pretty stupid things. Hurt a lot of people I shouldn't have." Then: "You want my own opinion, it's Flannery who killed the federal man and Flannery who killed Daly. People would just naturally think I did it. And then he'd have his wife all to himself again. And she wouldn't be sneaking off to see me."

"You mean that's still going on?"

He shook his head miserably. "I'm not saying it's right. I'm not saying he doesn't have a good reason to hate me for it. But the way he treats her—And we've been sweet on each other since she was in second grade and—" He shook his head again.

"You think Flannery knows she's still sneaking off?"

"It's a possibility. He seems to know everything else that goes on in town. Guess he feels that since he has all the money, it's his right to know or something."

I leaned back against the tree. "There's a man named Long. Seems when you robbed one of the banks, Flannery fired this Long's son. And now the son's practically out of money."

"Oh, shit," he said. "I didn't know that. That damned Flannery. That sounds like somethin' he'd do, fire somebody like that."

He didn't seem to understand that he just might have had something to do with that. "You didn't have to rob his bank, you know. That way his son would still have his job."

"Yeah, I suppose you're right if you look at it that way. But you look at it my way and you have to wonder how many ranches and farms Flannery would have foreclosed on if I hadn't robbed that bank."

I'd spoken to a lot of people and learned a lot of things in the past few days: "There's Nick Tremont. He claims you killed his son and since Sheriff Nordberg likes you and Jen so much, he wouldn't press any charges."

"His son tried to kill me because I was seeing the girl he used to court. It was on the up and up. She'd told him three or four months before I started seeing her that she didn't want to see him anymore. It was self-defense."

"From what I heard, you sure didn't do right by Loretta DeMeer." I hadn't talked to Loretta herself at that point, but that was one of the stories that folks trotted out whenever Chaney's name came up.

"Then you didn't hear it right."

He started to walk away, but I called out to him, "What about Jim Sloane and Tom Daly? Was that self-defense, too?" I don't know if I was trying to get some sense of him, or whether I was just cold and tired and lashing out a little bit.

He turned back and looked at me. "I'm sorry, Mr. Ford, but I don't know who they are."

"Jim was a federal agent, the first one sent here to try and track you down. Way I hear it, he was shot in the back within three days of arriving here. Tom was also a federal agent, and a good friend of mine. One of the deputies says he saw you shoot him."

Chaney looked at me, his eyes cold as the snow around us. "I never claimed to be an angel, Noah, but I'm not the devil some of them want to make me out to be. I steal from Flannery because he deserves it, and I killed Tremont in self-defense, but that's all that I've done. I've never murdered a man, I've never shot anyone in the back, and I did not kill either of your fellow agents. I guess it's up to you whether you believe me or not."

And then I asked him about blowing up the rear of that bank that night and robbing it.

"That wasn't me," Chaney said. "There was a witness that saw two men ridin' away from the bank right after it was robbed. But nobody'd believe it. They just figured it was me and that the witness was drunk and seein' things."

Two men. A huge explosion and fire . . . Connelly and Pepper.

Chapter 21

We avoided the main trail as long as we could. Between them, Jen and Mike seemed to know every twist and turn in the woods. By now, Connelly and Pepper had to know that the cave was empty. They would be backtracking, trying to find us. At least one of them would be riding the main trail. They'd be watching and listening for any sight or sound that would give away our location.

The temperature dropped. Stars swept across the dusk sky. This was three hours into our walk. We had a long way to go.

Poor little Clarice hadn't even lasted an hour. Jen carried her. She had to be tired. But after what Mike had said about never questioning her strength, she'd never let me share the load, though I'd asked her three times if she wanted me to take Clarice. Even in the dusk, her eyes had a fierceness. She didn't need to say anything. That glare of hers was answer enough.

But Clarice wasn't just a physical burden. She'd come out of her sleeping and start crying for her mommy. She'd even pound on Jen's chest, demanding to be put down so she could find her mommy. First she had denied the death; then she had acknowledged it; and finally she was angry and back to denying the death.

Jen's soothing words and soothing manners didn't have the effect they'd had earlier. But she wouldn't set Clarice down. And finally Clarice would slip back into sleep.

A couple of times I thought I heard a horse on the main trail. Both times I crept up to the edge of the woods. But I didn't see anything.

Much of the time the only sounds were the crunch of our footsteps on snow, the sound of our breathing, and the occasional whimpering of Clarice as she dealt with nightmares no child should ever have to confront.

I spent a good part of the time thinking about the people Mike and I had talked about. Somebody hated him. I wasn't sure he understood that. Both he and his sister seemed to see Mike's affairs with women as putting him in the "scoundrel" category. But men who do what he did are only "scoundrels" when their affairs don't touch you. Easy to laugh, even easy to admire in a certain nasty way.

Flannery hated him not only for business reasons— robbing his banks—but maybe even worse, from Flannery's point of view, because his wife had never given up on Mike.

Tremont's son had no right to draw down on Mike—that is, if Mike was telling the truth about the circumstances. If the girl had really broken it off with Tremont's son, then Mike wasn't sneaking off with her. But where your son was concerned, did you really care about that kind of truth? The only truth Tremont knew was that his son was dead at Mike's hands.

Then there was Long, with the son who couldn't find work. Everybody I'd talked to about Long talked about how crazy he got when he was drunk. Not difficult imagining him killing anybody, especially anybody he hated as much as he did Mike.

Sorting out the tangle wouldn't be easy. This case that was supposedly about federal bank notes being stolen—and thus federal investigators brought in—was really about the personal lives of everybody involved. And personal investigations were always a lot messier than professional ones.

I kept thinking of Jen's face whenever she stood close to her brother. Her love for him was both touching and scary. Touching for the obvious reason but also scary because she refused to hold him to what he'd done. What if it turned out that he had killed Daly and the man before him? Even though I had finally came to believe his story, what if I later found out he was lying?

Who would Jen back in a showdown? Her brother or the law? I wasn't sure I wanted to know the answer to that.

So we trudged on, night settling in, the wind down, no fresh snow. Every once in a while, Mike would start joking with Jen. I started wondering about it. I'd taken Jen's word that he was a decent young man who'd only tried to help the people in his valley.

But he was pretty damned jaunty for somebody with all his troubles.

By six o'clock, according to my railroad watch read by the light of the moon, I needed to stop and rest. Jen's steps were dragging. Clarice slept in her arms but was held lower and looser than she had been at the start. Even Mike had slowed noticeably.

I decided to call uncle first. "Why don't we stop? Mike can pass around his canteen and that jerky he said he had."

"I'm not tired," Jen said. "But then I'm not as old as you are."

Mike said, "She was always like this."

I laughed. "That, I don't doubt."

Mike said, "Sis, you know darned well you're ready to drop. Let's do what Ford, here, suggests and rest a while."

The way they treated each other was with a kind of rough tenderness. They would take care of each other to the death if necessary. That was a good kind of partnership to have, whether it was spouses, kin, or just friends.

No significant wind and no snow at all. We could keep moving as long as we had the stamina. And the blessing of the moon. Light bloomed broken down through the boughs and branches of the forest, pointing our way.

"Maybe they won't find us," Mike said as we cut along the trail.

"They'll do their best."

I sensed his eyes on me. "You having second thoughts about my story?"

"Maybe a little."

"I told you the truth."

"Maybe."

"Well, thanks for making me a suspect again."

"You asked me if I was having second thoughts. I have second thoughts about everybody in every investigation. Having them is part of my job."

He laughed; it was a harsh sound. "You trust your father?"

"I did while he was alive."

"You ever have a wife?"

"Yep."

"You trust her?"

"Nope. She didn't even trust herself."

"You're a strange one, you know that, Ford?"

"Not the first time I've heard that one."

"What'll you tell Nordberg when we get back to town?"

"Won't tell him anything. Just hand you over. Which is what I told him I'd do."

"How about Connelly and Pepper? What happens to them?"

"Them, we'll have to see about." Then: "We've talked enough. No sense helping them find us."

He muttered something I wasn't able to hear. Then he fell back. Spoke softly to his sister. "You got quite the man there."

"He's trying to help us."

"Not the way he's talking to me, he isn't. He's changed his mind. He thinks I killed Daly and the other federal man."

I stopped, turned: "Be quiet, Mike. Don't make it easy for them."

"See? You see, Jen?" As if I'd just proved his point by speaking up the way I had.

We fell into silence; our pace picked up. Every so often an odd noise would freeze all of us in place. Then, once we were sure the noise wasn't Connelly and Pepper, we moved on.

A break in the timber gave us a look at the moon hanging above the ragged chain of mountains. I suppose we're each struck in our own way by the timeless and almost alien beauty of that landscape.

Clarice woke up. She needed to pee. We all did. We took turns. A couple times I thought I heard something. It was awkward raising steam against a tree with one hand and clutching my rifle with the other.

Then Mike was carrying Clarice.

Jen caught up to me. "Mike says you don't believe him anymore."

"I want to and in the end I probably will believe him. But I always have second thoughts."

"If you're such a good detective why would you have doubts?"

I sighed. "Look, Jen, as I told Mike, all I'm going to do is turn him over to Nordberg. He can take it from there. That's all that's going to happen. You trust Nordberg, don't you?"

"Of course."

"Then there's nothing to worry about. We'll both work on finding the man we want and I doubt that'll be your brother." Then: "Jen, the more we talk like this, the more likely they are to find us. Why help them?"

Around seven o'clock, the wind started getting harsh again, meaning we could talk in soft voices again.

We stopped. Mike and I found fir trees and stripped away enough material to build another lean-to. In case we decided to spend the night there—or if the weather decided to force us to stay—we had something to put against the dark gods.

On our last trip for branches, Mike stopped me and said, "I'm nervous about going into town."

"You put up a good front."

He shrugged.

"I'm like Sis, I guess. She's not as tough as she pretends to be." Then: "I'll own up to the bank robberies. I damned well wanted to stop Flannery from getting all that land back and I'm proud to say I did a fair job of it. But I'm against anybody getting hurt. I left two of his banks because the only way I could get the money was to shoot somebody and I wouldn't do it."

"A lot of people think you killed those men. That needs to be straightened out. I'll help with that and so will Nordberg."

"That's why I'm getting nervous about heading to town."

"You took a lot of chances robbing banks."

"You don't know Flannery. You don't live here. You don't know all the good people he hurt. He didn't leave me much choice."

The cry—and it was a cry, not a scream—came from the approximate position where we'd planned on throwing in for a while.

Mike and I damned near knocked each other over trying to get up trail to see what was going on.

By the time we got there, we could hear Jen calling out Clarice's name.

Jen was walking up and down the shadowy trail, so frantic it didn't seem like the tough Jen she usually was.

"What happened?" I asked when I reached her.

"She just got hysterical. She said she wanted to find her mommy, wanted to go back to the cabin. And before I knew it, she started running toward the main trail. I ran after her but I tripped and hit my head on a rock."

Not till then did I notice the small but nasty bulb on the right side of her head. A trickle of blood snaked from it.

"We have to find her," she said.

We went single file up trail, each of us calling out her name, scanning the dense woods on either side of us. The eyes of a dozen creatures followed us. A raccoon sat close to the path watching each one of us from behind his black bandit mask. At that moment I wished that I knew those woods as well as he did.

"I'm so damned clumsy," Jen said.

"Don't start that," I said. "This isn't your fault. She's a little girl who saw her mother raped and murdered. She's liable to do anything."

"Well, if I hadn't tripped she wouldn't have gotten away."

"That's another thing about Jen," Mike said. "She's all right unless something goes wrong. Then she usually blames herself." Then: "There's a path over there I'm gonna try. You keep on the trail here."

He vanished into the trees off the path we were on.

"I don't know how you can even *think* he killed anybody. Look how helpful he is with Clarice."

"There's no time for that now, Jen. We need to find Clarice."

Jen and I kept repeating Clarice's name. We sounded increasingly frenzied. The prospect of a little girl lost in those woods—

There is a truth among saloonkeepers that a man is at his most dangerous when he's been betrayed by his woman.

That is also true about people who are responsible for children who have suddenly disappeared. A real madness sets in. Hard enough to think about adults you care for falling into dark clutches. But when a vulnerable child is in possible peril—

In the war you would see battles that spread to farmhouses. You would see the mothers in gingham searching desperately for their little ones before the soldiers were pushed back to their front yards. Their voices were terrible to hear—that mixture of fear and terror and hope as the guns and cries of war came nearer and nearer. And somewhere their little ones lost.

We spent the next fifteen minutes on and off the path. Once we thought we heard something—neither of us quite sure what it was—something like a little girl's cry. But we decided it was an animal and then continued on searching.

It must have been twenty minutes before we came to the mouth of the path. Small sobs exploded in Jen's throat every few minutes. I sensed she was punishing herself.

She tripped again. Ordinarily, she'd probably have

resented me picking her up. She was the kind who wanted to pick herself up. But there wasn't any time for her to find her strength and then climb back. And that bump on her head must have still been hurting.

I got her to her feet.

"I don't know how I could've let her out of my sight like this."

"Don't be stupid. You didn't hit your head again?"

But instead of answering me, she called out Clarice's name again and began stumbling forward on the path. She slipped once, dropping to one knee. But she'd be damned if I helped her up again. She did it herself.

We could hear Mike somewhere in the darkness west of the trail. His voice had taken on the same edge as ours. Increasingly scared, increasingly frustrated.

I was right behind Jen as we approached the opening of the path that would take us to the mountain trail most people used in their ascent. By that point, both Jen and I seemed to have a new energy borne of pure fear for Clarice. I kept playing the same possibilities over and over, everything from mountain lions to outcroppings where a little girl might plunge a hundred feet to her death.

Jen reached the trail before I did.

I could hear horses nearby.

She mustn't have seen anything at first. She ran out onto the trail. She looked back down and then quickly up the trail. Then her body sort of jerked backward, as if somebody had punched her.

I heard her gasp and then say, "Oh, Lord."

I took the last few steps to reach her.

And before I could quite see what she was responding to, a harsh male voice said: "I think this is the little girl you're looking for, isn't it, Ford?" It was Connelly talking.

Then I saw them, Connelly and Pepper. Connelly had grabbed Clarice. She must have wandered onto the main trail when she ran off. Her eyes were luminous with terror.

He had her in front of him on his saddle, big mittened hand covering her mouth.

Pepper had a Colt on Mike.

Mike said: "I found Clarice but Connelly grabbed her before I could."

Pepper laughed: "And then we found both of them. Worked out real nice."

Connelly laughed. "That Mike's a real hero, though, isn't he? How much of that bank money you stole did you hide away somewhere?"

"None," Mike snapped.

Connelly said: "I got to give you one thing, kid. You sure have a way with the ladies. But if a certain man I know ever finds out that you were with *his* lady you're in bigger trouble than ever. And I think you know who I'm talking about."

"Shut up!" Mike half-shouted. He sounded as much nervous as angry. Made me wonder who Connelly was talking about.

But Connelly was finished stirring up Mike. "If you'd be kind enough to empty your weapons and then throw the bullets into the woods, I'd be most appreciative."

Pepper: "You do that and we'll hand the girl back. And then we'll take the killer here into town."

Jen glanced at me. She wanted to fight. She'd be

angry that I didn't agree. But Connelly and Pepper were running this particular face-off. They had the girl and they had Mike.

"I want your guarantee you won't hurt him," I snapped.

"You're a bossy bastard, you know that, Noah? And it's not just me and Pepper say that, either. A lot of men in the agency do. 'He's a nice fella, that Noah Ford,' they say, 'but he thinks he runs the whole show.' They say that a lot, don't they, Pepper?"

"They sure do. You mention the name Noah Ford and that's all you hear. How he always puts himself in charge of everything."

"But this time, Noah, we're in charge. And we're telling you to empty your guns and then drop them. And then throw the bullets into the woods. Same with the gal. You do the same, miss."

Jen glared at me. Then glared back at Connelly.

"Takes a tough man to hold on to a little girl the way you are."

"You can't insult me, miss, because I don't give a shit whether you like me or not. And when you don't care what people think of you, you can do just about anything you care to."

Clarice started wrestling around under his grip. Forcing him to demonstrate that she wasn't as easy to hold on to as he'd just insinuated.

I had to make a decision, and I had to make it fast. I knew that I couldn't trust Connelly and Pepper to keep their word. They were a lot of things, but honest wasn't one of them. But what choice did I have? If we tried to fight, we'd be killed before we even got off a single shot.

On the other hand, I didn't really think they would kill us, not now that they had Chaney. He'd be a witness against them, and even two senators couldn't save Connelly and Pepper if they were accused of killing a federal agent. So they had a choice, too. They could kill all of us, including Chaney, and lose the glory that would come with taking him in alive, or they could leave Jen, Clarice, and me alive, knowing that it would take a long time for us to get back to town—and we might not even make it.

Not much of a choice. One way we died for sure, and one way we had a small hope.

I did the only thing I could. I emptied the carbine and then I emptied my .44. I hurled everything into the woods.

"Now you, ma'am," Connelly said.

He was enjoying himself. I wondered if this was as much fun as taking a broom to a defenseless woman. Or killing a little boy. Probably not.

"We don't have any choice," I said to Jen.

She frowned at me, then set about doing what I just had. But she did it at her own pace, purposely irritating Connelly and Pepper.

She hurled her bullets into the woods.

"You've got a nice throwing arm there, lady. You could be an outfielder."

He encircled Clarice with his right arm and then carefully climbed down from his horse. Once they were on the ground, Clarice tried to kick him. "I don't know what it is about gals around here. That Jen gal there, she'd put a knife in my back first chance she got. And this little one here—"

He shoved Clarice toward Jen. The girl, sobbing

suddenly, fell into Jen's arms. Jen picked her up, holding her tight.

Pepper kept his carbine trained on Mike.

"I want an understanding here," I said.

"Yeah," Pepper said, "and what would that be?"

"That would be that Mike is alive when you get him back to town."

"You sure worry a lot about a cold-blooded killer," Connelly said.

"I want him alive," I said. "And you better remember that."

"See, Noah, there you go again," Connelly said. "Bein' the boss. Tellin' me this and tellin' me that. And now you're threatening me on top of it. I don't like that. And I'll bet Pepper doesn't like it, either." He called over his shoulder. "Isn't that right, Pepper?"

"I don't like threats and I don't like Ford."

Connelly smiled. "Now there's a vote of confidence for you, Mr. Ford."

"Just remember what I said about getting Mike back safe, Connelly. I'm going to hold you responsible."

In the moonlight, Mike's young face looked sad and scared. He had to know that these men would shoot him for anything he did that so much as irritated them.

"I'll see you in town," he said. His voice was shaking.

Jen's attention was divided. Clarice was still crying, the sound muffled because her face was buried in Jen's shoulder. But Jen also wanted to comfort her brother in some way, too. Reassure him so he wouldn't be so afraid. But all she managed was: "I'll see you in town, Mike. You'll get a fair hearing. Noah will see to it."

Pepper dropped down from his saddle, crunched through the snow to Mike. The soaring mountains outlined in the moonlight, the blue-tinted snow, three deer crossing the mountain path just below us—an ideal picture of the mountains. Connelly and Pepper shouldn't have been in that picture at all. They were vulgar, profane.

Mike started to talk but before he got three words out, Pepper whipped out a pair of handcuffs and clamped them on Mike's wrists. Then Pepper went back to his horse and produced a good stretch of rope. He tied this around Mike's neck. Pepper went back to his horse and climbed up in the saddle. Connelly helped Mike up into Pepper's saddle, in the front position. If Mike tried to escape, he wouldn't get far. The rope wasn't very long.

"Probably be tomorrow before you folks get back to town," Pepper said. "Be a hell of a cold walk for ya."

Connelly came over to me. I knew what to expect. With Pepper's carbine on me, Connelly could do what he wanted. I just hoped he didn't break anything. We had a long cold walk back to town ahead of us.

He put his fist wrist-deep into my stomach and just when I was buckling, he brought his right fist up and caught me square on the jaw. When I lunged for him, Pepper sent a bullet searing right past my shoulder.

"You try to hit him again, Ford," Pepper said, "I'll kill you on the spot."

Connelly went for my groin with his knee and then when I was in enough writhing pain there on the ground, he decided to stomp on my hand. His spur jangled as he raised his boot for the stomping.

And then I didn't give a damn. Let Pepper kill me. Right then all that mattered was getting to Connelly. Just when he was ready to crush my gun hand, I reached up and grabbed his boot with enough force to jerk him off balance. Then I was on my feet and ready to get some vengeance. I slammed a fist to his forehead and then returned the favor to his groin.

I was just ready to start stomping him once I had him on his knees and ready to spill over backward when Pepper must have sighted his rifle because suddenly Jen was there, standing in front of me and screaming, "You'll have to shoot me to get to him! Are you ready to do that?"

Any other time, I would have smiled at Jen's words. Anybody who'd done to a woman what Pepper had done to Clarice's mother wouldn't hesitate to merely shoot a woman. That was a nice, clean, civilized job compared to what he'd done back there in that cabin where Clarice and her mother and brother had been staying.

But for right then I was grateful to Jen for so foolishly shielding me. Pepper probably understood that he might get away with killing Mike in cold blood—he might even get away with killing me that way, too—but killing Jen? Nordberg wouldn't stand for that. He'd make Connelly and Pepper pay for sure.

"Put the rifle down," Connelly said, rising uncomfortably to his feet, grimacing from groin pain every few seconds. "Let's just get the hell out of here."

He walked bowlegged over to his horse. Any other time watching him walk would have been funny, but now it was just grotesque. Like Connelly himself.

"G'bye, Jen," Mike said from atop Pepper's horse.

"You'll be fine, Mike," she said. "I know you will be."

Connelly laughed, though pain was evident in his voice.

"That's right, little brother. We'll take real good care of you." Then to me: "This isn't over between us. You know that, don't you?"

I didn't say anything. I was tired of all his bad-guy bullshit. There comes a point when people like Connelly talked tough just to hear their own voices.

Then they rode off.

Chapter 22

Our first thought was to start after them right away. But then I suggested we try and get some sleep and then set out.

At first, Jen balked. I didn't blame her. If Mike was my brother, I'd want to go after them immediately.

But he wasn't my brother and so I could look at things with a clearer eye. Clarice had already fallen into a fitful sleep. And Jen and I were tired, too. Why not use the lean-to Mike and I had thrown together?

Jen needed to curse somebody so she cursed me. I didn't know what I was doing. I didn't give a damn about her brother. I was going to get reprimanded when she wrote a letter to my boss.

But after she choked down a piece of bread and positioned herself next to Clarice under the lean-to, she was asleep in just a few minutes. She worked up some good snoring pretty fast, too.

For a time, I couldn't sleep. I dwelt on some of those bad memories that never seem fresher or more urgent than when you're lying awake like that. People who hated me; things they'd said. People I hated; things I'd said. People who'd failed me; people I'd failed. Nothing about the present time, nothing about Jen or Clarice or Mike or Connelly. Just things from the past. Too bad they couldn't be cut out with a scalpel.

Then I finally slept, but on my arm, crooked, so that it hurt some when I woke up.

When I finally fought my eyes open, I had one of those moments when I wasn't sure where I was.

Darkness. Snow. Broken moonlight.

"Let's get going."

I raised my head. Jen carried my rifle in one hand and was holding Clarice over her shoulder with the other. I took the rifle and loaded it with the extra bullets I kept in my pocket.

I walked down trail and pissed and came back and said, "I'll take her."

"I wouldn't want to make you actually work."

Still pissed off.

"Even if you didn't, I needed to rest."

"Maybe you're too old for this job."

"I'm forty-one. I've probably got a few good years left."

"They'll kill him."

"Maybe not. I warned them."

"Yeah, and they really looked scared."

I glared at her. "What the hell is wrong with you?"

"I'm tired of weak men. I've never met a so-called man who could measure up to my father."

"Lead on, General."

She led on.

When we'd gone no more than ten yards, she turned around, Clarice in her arms and said, "You could've done something."

"I tried. But it's hard to do anything when somebody's pointing a carbine at you, which, in case you hadn't noticed, Pepper was doing."

"You're a federal man. That's supposed to mean something."

I laughed bitterly. "Mean what? That bullets don't hurt us? You're being stupid, Jen. I'm sorry they took Mike. I hope they take him in alive. I warned them."

As soon as I said it, I knew I shouldn't have. I'd just handed her a weapon.

"The big brave federal man warned them." She smirked. "I could've done that myself. It doesn't take any guts to just warn somebody—especially if you don't back it up with anything."

She turned around and started walking.

There were birds before there was light. There were birds and then there were wolves and then there were more birds. And then there was that streaky half-light. By then, Clarice had been set down and was walking just behind Jen.

The sun was starting to send brilliant lances across the still-dark sky. Stars were starting to vanish. A mist lay across the moon. Between our own footfalls you could hear the animals in the snow in the forest on either side of us.

I was working over her remark about her father. That went a long way in explaining why she was still not married. We talk about mamas' boys a lot but we never pay much attention to women who are under the sway of their fathers. And the sway can imprison them even beyond the grave. I knew I wasn't tough but I also knew I wasn't weak. I did my job and I'd survived quite a few different times that other men wouldn't have. So her words stung. I didn't have much of a life except for my job and when somebody attacked me for not doing that well—

"I need to do my business."

That was the official way we now discussed toilet needs. "My business." Clarice said it curtly, then headed off into the woods.

"Don't go very far," Jen said.

"She'll be all right."

"Thanks for the reassurance."

I smiled and the smile and the ripe golden dawn starting to break on the horizon were enough to stop me from sulking anymore.

"You calmed down any?"

"I'm not up to talking right now."

"Glad you don't hold grudges."

That got me a scowl.

I did some mountain gazing. The snow, blue gone with the night sky, was slowly becoming white again. The lowest clouds on the mountain were starting to thin. Somebody down mountain rang a breakfast bell. There was a chance that somebody who lived higher up than where we stood, tucked away somewhere, might come down to town in a wagon and tell us to hop on.

Clarice came back and said, "I saw a mama deer."

"A doe."

"How come they call them that?"

"Maybe you should ask the federal man."

I looked at Clarice. "She's mad at me."

"She called you a name last night. I told her I liked you."

"I appreciate that. And I like you, too."

"How come she's mad at you?"

"I guess you'll have to ask her, Clarice."

She looked up at Jen and said, "How come you're mad at him?"

Then Jen surprised me and I assumed she surprised Clarice, too. "I'm just worried, honey. About my brother Mike. And I needed somebody to take it out on." Her gaze rested on me. "Sometimes I'm petty."

"Gosh, I hadn't noticed that," I said.

"You're supposed to be gracious when somebody's apologizing."

"What's 'gracious' mean?" Clarice asked.

"It means you're supposed to be nice about it when somebody says they're sorry about something."

"Oh. You mean you're sorry for calling him that name?"

"Yes." She laughed. "And it wasn't a very bad name, anyway."

"I'll bet."

"So, I'm sorry, Noah."

"Thank you for saying that."

"Can we start walking again?" Clarice asked. "It gets cold when you just stand in one place."

Jen studied my face for a time and then looked down at Clarice, who stood next to her, and said: "Let's go, honey."

We held up pretty well most of the morning. We ate jerky as we walked and shared what was left of the canteen. The kid had slipped into herself again. She rarely said anything. I hated to think of what she was reliving in her mind over and over.

Around noon, the sky started turning gray again.

The morning had glowed with sunlight. The deer to the west, and there must have been a hundred of them spread out over the long slope, noted our passage with that quick animal curiosity that never seems to last more than a few seconds.

Clarice just gave out. She'd been walking upfront with Jen, who had slowed down so that Clarice could maintain her normal pace, when she just tripped and flopped down face-first onto the snowy trail.

Jen and I were over her in seconds. I grabbed her underneath her arms, picked her up, held her in front of Jen for inspection.

"You just tired, honey?"

Clarice just nodded. Then she started crying. "I want to see my mommy."

"I know you do, sweetie."

"Can we go back to that cabin where Mommy is?"

Jen's eyes flicked to mine.

"We'll be there by nightfall, hon."

Clarice yawned. "I'm sleepy."

"I'll carry her," I said.

After finishing off the canteen, we started walking again. We wouldn't want for water. Not with all the snow around us.

You could see the tracks left by Connelly and Pepper. By now they'd be in town. I wondered what they'd tell Nordberg. Connelly was always good and quick with stories for any situation. They'd likely be gone by the time we got there. Chuck Gage had been afraid of them. I doubted he'd gone to the sheriff's office. Connelly and Pepper knew their time with the agency was over. They'd know I'd come after them for what they'd done in that cabin. For people like them, there were banks to rob and con games to play and Mexico and South America to hide in if things got very bad.

Mike was another matter. Nordberg and I between us had to find out who'd actually killed Jim Sloane. And who'd killed Tom Daly.

But even after we found the killer, Mike was headed for prison. The James Gang always said they were robbing banks and trains for the sake of the people, too. You might have noticed that the law hadn't looked kindly on their pleas. As much of a greedy bastard as Flannery might be, Mike had no legal right to do what he'd done. His best hope was of finding a sympathetic jury that would be swayed by this homegrown Robin Hood legend.

The snow started about an hour into the afternoon. A confetti snow. The temperature drop had its effect on the bones. You have arthritis or rheumatism on a long, cold walk and your bones begin to remind you of who is in charge of your body. The bones ache, they burn and there isn't a damned thing you can do about it except waste your money on some kind of quack patent medicine.

Jen talked Clarice into singing some songs. They both sounded girlie and sweet.

I broke away once to find food for the night. The jerky was about gone. One thing I wasn't, was a hunter. Three rabbits escaped me before I was finally able to shoot one.

I carried it along on the walk, keeping it as well

hidden as I could. I didn't know how Clarice was doing and I wasn't sure she'd want to see anything dead. I trailed behind a good twenty feet.

But of course that concern became moot just as the long shadows from the mountains started to wrap us in their cold dark shroud. The sunset was almost the same color as the drops of blood from the rabbit.

We came up over a little hill and Jen stopped suddenly, swooped up Clarice and ran back to me.

She stood Clarice down and said, "Wait here, honey."

She grabbed my arm and took me over to the side of the trail. It was almost dark, the dense woods on either side becoming shadowy walls.

"What's going on?" I asked.

"Down there. There's a dead man—he looks dead, anyway—in the middle of the trail. And there are two horses. I didn't see anything else. The horses looked like the ones Connelly and Pepper were riding."

I walked the rabbit over into the shadows and kicked snow over it. Then I stuck a long twig up to mark the spot. Too easy to lose without some way of identifying the spot.

Clarice hugged Jen around the waist. They both looked like statues.

This time of day, with shadows playing games, it was easy to mistake what you were seeing. Especially if you were worried about somebody the way Jen was worried about her brother.

I had to damned near walk to the man before I believed it was a man. I walked around, looking everything over, trying to imagine what had happened there.

When I came back, I said, "I'll go down there now. You wait here."

Jen clutched my arm. "I really am sorry for what I said, Noah."

I patted her hand.

"Is it Mike?"

"I don't know yet. I didn't go all the way down. There may be a shooter in the woods. I wanted to grab my carbine."

She gripped my wrist.

"I'm sorry I'm not handling this better."

"You're handling it just fine."

I walked over and grabbed my carbine. Then I walked down to where the two horses and the man waited in the sudden wind. I'd lied to her. It was Mike I'd seen all right and he was dead all right. I couldn't lie to her again, though. This time I'd have to tell her the truth for sure.

Chapter 23

Not much doubt about it being Mike. He'd been shot at least twice in the back with a shotgun.

I looked at the two horses. I picked up their reins and took them over to a tree where I tethered them to heavy branches.

I might never have found them if Connelly hadn't started moaning.

I hadn't really counted on anybody being in the woods. But that's where the moaning came from and so that's where I went, gun drawn.

It wasn't a path so much as a narrow clearing that ran straight into the woods. I had a carbine and a pistol then. The dark didn't scare me. But not knowing what was going on did. This thing didn't figure at all.

Low pine branches sprinkled snow on me as I brushed against them. The moaning came and went. When I saw them I felt even more spooked. This didn't make any sense at all.

If they'd decided to kill Mike and leave him on the trail that way, then what were they doing lying on the ground there? The only light on their faces was moonlight patterned through the pines.

I walked around in the bloody shadows. The only sound in the lee of the looming lonely mountain was my crunching footsteps.

I knelt down next to Pepper. He'd vomited all over his chest. The stink was bad. I tried his neck and wrist for a pulse. Nothing. He was dead for sure. For the first time the woods seemed dark and dangerous to me. An explanation for this situation was forming in my mind. Something to do with these woods.

I rolled Pepper over. He'd been shot in the back several times. I rolled him back over so I could go through his pockets.

"You steal from dead men, Ford?" Connelly, his voice thin and raspy in the cold air.

I said nothing. I kept turning Pepper's pockets out.

"It isn't easy for me to talk, Ford. You hear what I asked you?"

I was finished with Pepper. I got up and walked over to Connelly.

He had propped himself up against a tree. He didn't look all that bad. It was like him to be the survivor.

"It's cold," he said. "I don't suppose you'd help me get to town?"

"What happened?"

"You didn't answer my question."

"You didn't answer mine, either, Connelly."

He coughed. "Somebody shot us from the woods. We were headed back to town. I didn't get a chance to see who it was. I knew I'd freeze to death out in the open tonight. I crawled in here. Figured I'd hear

you and the woman when you came down the trail."
He coughed again. "Help me up, huh?"

"Pepper didn't see anything, either?"

"Nah. I don't even know how he was able to crawl
in here with me. I thought he was dead back on the
trail. Now how about a hand up?"

"Mike die right off, did he?"

"Not right off. He was crying like a little baby.
You should've heard him, Ford. Sickening. Those
punks today wouldn't last a month, goin' through
the shit we been through."

He moaned again.

"Where'd you get hit?"

"I took two shots high on the shoulder. A doc can
fix me up fine. All you need to do is put me on my
horse. Now help me up?"

I raised my .44.

"Hey, what the hell's this, Ford? You got no call
to shoot me. We didn't kill the punk there. The
shooter did."

"Which one of you put the broom up her?"

He started to say something, a lie, and then
stopped.

"You saw her, huh?"

"Yeah. I saw her."

"That kid—the little boy—that was strictly an accident. We shoved him is all and he hit his head. We
don't go around killing little kids. You know us better than that."

"Which one of you used the broom on her?"

"Pepper. I told him not to do it. You know I
wouldn't do anything like that. Pepper was crazy.
You know that. I screwed her. I'll admit that. But that

broom shit—that was all Pepper. Like I said—" He coughed. "You know how Pepper was. He liked hurtin' women. He'd screw 'em and then he would hurt them. Her, he hurt bad."

He was babbling, scared. He saw what I was going to do. "You a Catholic?"

"Most of the time."

"You know what I'm doing right now? Right here talking to you? I'm shitting my pants. I never even done that in the war. But I'm scared, Noah. I never seen you like this before." Coughed again. "You kill a man in cold blood, you'll go straight to hell. I'm a Catholic, too, don't forget that. That's what our religion teaches us, Noah. We kill somebody in cold blood and we go to hell."

"It'll be worth it."

I put one bullet in his eye and one bullet in his heart, then I raised the gun and put two shots in his forehead.

I went through his pockets, just like I had gone through Pepper's a few minutes ago, just like I was trained to do. Half the time anything I find I just throw away. But you can't be sure what might be in those pockets so you look, you search. And sometimes you get lucky. I didn't get lucky. Not that night. He hadn't been lying about shitting his pants. But the animals that would rend him later on that night wouldn't care. They didn't have what you might call delicate palates.

I walked out of the dark woods, picked Mike up, and slung him over my shoulder. I felt cold and sick the way I used to get in the war sometimes. And it wasn't just the weather.

When I reached the top of the hill where Jen had spotted the two horses and Mike's body, she started walking slowly toward me, Clarice at her side. Then she broke and started running so fast toward me that she nearly fell over twice. With the dying light, the snow was glazing again.

I didn't say anything to her. What was there to say? She ran up to the horse that carried her brother. I stopped right there and just watched her.

She took his face in her hands and kissed it with great reverence. Then she began touching her face against his, the way animals rub against each other. And finally she took his face again and kissed him on the mouth.

Clarice came up and took my hand. We stood there together just watching Jen. Finally Clarice broke away, ran to Jen, who had now fallen to her knees, sobbing. Clarice came up and slid her arms around Jen and held her very much the way Jen had held Clarice the night before, in the cabin where her mother lay.

At first I thought that Jen might push her away but she suddenly embraced her and they held each other for a long time.

It was time to get back to town. Straight through. No stops except for what the preachers always call "biological necessities."

I mounted the horse with Mike on it and then said, "We can make town by midnight if we leave now."

They were both still crying, still clinging to each

other but more loosely now. Jen got up so abruptly I thought she was angry. She stormed over to the other horse, grabbed Clarice, set her up in the saddle and then climbed up herself. She looked back at me and said, "C'mon, Noah, I just want to get the hell out of here."

It was night by then. In the starlight Jen looked wan but pretty. Clarice looked happy to be on a horse. Every so often she'd tug on the reins. Being a big girl.

We didn't speak for maybe ten minutes, till Jen said: "How about Connelly and Pepper?"

"Same man killed Mike and Pepper."

"What about Connelly?"

We rode at a good but easy clip. Talking was no problem.

"I decided to save you folks a trial."

She just nodded and kissed the top of Clarice's cap.

"Why'd you kill him?"

"It's an old tradition in the justice code. Called General Principles."

"General Principles?"

"Sometimes there are people you can't kill for any one specific thing. But you can kill them for things they've done in general."

"So you executed him."

I changed the subject. "Whoever shot everybody tonight figures Nordberg and the county attorney will drop everything, not pursue it. Figure it was just somebody who had it in for Connelly and Pepper and killed your brother so he couldn't testify against him."

"You got anybody in mind who that might be?"

"Not yet," I said. "But give me a couple days."

PART THREE

Chapter 24

I'm not sure that small towns need those new inventions called telephones. Word spreads fast all by itself.

We hadn't been back in town with Mike Chaney's body fifteen minutes before the street outside the funeral home was filled with a crowd of maybe a hundred people.

They had a good day for gawking. The sunlight had lanced through the white clouds and the sky was a light blue. The temperature was in the thirties. Not exactly tropical, but given the past two days, damned comfortable for being outdoors.

Sheriff Nordberg and I were upstairs in the funeral parlor while Doc Tomkins was downstairs examining the body.

Just before you went in the room where the wakes were held, there was an area with a horsehair couch and a small table and chairs. This was likely the area where the family met the other mourners.

But Nordberg wasn't mourning. He was angry.

"I just can't credence our own government hiring

a couple of thugs like Connelly and Pepper. Lawmen are supposed to be—law abiding."

I shrugged. "They knew all the bad guys and a lot of the bad guys trusted them. That was how they got their information for Washington. They could eat, drink, and whore right next to the bad guys. And pick up a lot of information while they were doing it."

"Yeah. And look what they did to that poor woman in the cabin. Where's the little girl, anyway?"

"Jen took her home. Give her a bath. Put her to bed. Then fix her a good meal when she wakes up. I hope Jen gets a bath and a meal, too. I hired a couple of men to go out to the cabin and get the girl's mother and brother. We'll give them a decent burial here. This has been hard on Clarice. She deserves seeing them buried proper."

He grimaced. "Hard on the whole town. You see the people in the street?"

"Yeah."

"That crowd'll double in size by midafternoon and on toward evening it'll triple. He was their hero."

"They didn't mind him chasing after married women?"

He smiled and shook his head. "Anybody else, they would've run out of town. The British like to call men like that 'bounders.' Well, around here bounders get run out of town. But with Chaney— they just didn't want to hear about it. Somebody'd bring the subject up—how he was seen up in the haymow with so-and-so—and they'd just turn away. They saw Mike as their hero. They didn't want to hear anything that took away from that."

He leaned back in his chair, his size imposing in

that tiny room where, if you listened carefully, you could still hear the sobbing of mourners, ghost cries that had saturated the air in that house, just as much as the cloying sweet scent of flowers had.

"Not everybody liked him. Somebody in this town killed him."

"What makes you so sure of that? Somebody killed him but I think who you mean by that is Flannery."

"That scare you?"

"I've got a family to support. You want to know how fast he could get me fired?"

"Would the folks around here stand for that?"

"What choice would they have?"

I reached in my pocket and took out the small notebook I usually carried. "Well, it's not just Flannery I'm talking about. Here are some names, if you'd like to see them. It's not necessarily one of them but it's a start."

He took my notebook, looked it over. In the office to our left, a woman said, "Did you see the livery bill for last month?"

"He must think we live in Denver," another woman said, "the prices he charges."

"Well, Doc certainly isn't going to stand for this."

Even in the face of death the daily work goes on, two women bitching about the monthly livery bill. Nordberg got my attention again.

"You going to start bothering them, I suppose?" Nordberg said, handing back my notebook.

"You don't want to find out who killed the first federal man and then Daly?"

"You don't care about Connelly and Pepper?" He smiled.

"Not so's you'd notice."

"You wouldn't have killed either one of them, would you?"

"If you're going in that direction, why not say I killed both of them?"

"Did you?"

"I wanted to but somebody else got to them first."

He straightened his string tie and sat up straight. I wondered if he'd suddenly seen a pretty lady. "Well, I'll help you."

"I was hoping you'd say that."

"You take a few of the names to check out and I'll take the rest." Then: "I'm sorry I'm a coward. A man doesn't like to think of himself that way. If you wouldn't mind—"

"Sure. I'll take Flannery."

"He won't be easy."

"Neither will I." I picked up the makings I'd left on the table. "And you're not a coward. Like you say, you have a family. You have to live here. I don't. I have no family and when this is all done, I get on a train and clear out. I've got the easy part."

"I appreciate you taking Flannery like that."

I stood up. "Now it's my turn for a bath and some good sleep. I should be up by late afternoon. I'll go over to the bank and talk to Flannery."

"You have to get past Mrs. Milligan first."

"Who's Mrs. Milligan?"

He smiled. "Let's just say she scares the hell out of every man in this county. But you'll find out for yourself." He smiled some more and then went downstairs to see what Doc was learning from his examination of the body.

When I reached the front steps, I saw that Nordberg's prediction had come true. The crowd had grown.

I stared at them and they stared back at me. They'd know I hadn't killed their hero. But they just might be thinking that if I hadn't come to town somehow that hero would still be alive.

People need somebody to blame when things go wrong, especially when death's involved.

Mrs. Milligan's desk was on a riser set directly in front of the circular vault that had been built into the wall. I had been escorted there by an elderly bank guard who said, "She's got a head cold so be careful."

I guess I was expecting a behemoth. You know how you imagine things based on somebody's comments.

Mrs. Milligan weighed, at the outside, ninety pounds. Her gray hair was pulled back into a bun so severe you could see stretch marks on the side of her face. She wore a black dress with a black collar and black-framed glasses almost as tiny as her black eyes. The sharp nose and the huge drooping growth to the right of her mouth gave her the look of a witch. The tiny eyes winced when I came into their view, as if they had just seen something that gave them profound displeasure. She sneezed with such force that her glasses flew from her face and landed on the desktop. The eyes dared me to show amusement.

"God bless you."

She picked up her glasses and said, "You don't

look like the sort who has any right to use the Lord's name."

"And you must be Mrs. Milligan."

Her seventy-year-old face broke into a leer. "You've heard the stories, then, have you? That's how the teacher threatens her students. She told me that at the church picnic this summer. She just says, 'You want me to send you to see Mrs. Milligan?' She says I scare them more than Geronimo."

Then she put her glasses back on with knotty little hands and said: "Why do you want to see Mr. Flannery?"

"I'm afraid I can't discuss it."

"Then *I'm* afraid you can't see him."

I held up my badge.

She said: "Is that thing real?"

"Uh-huh."

"What if I still won't let you see him?"

"Then I'll just walk over to that office that says 'President' on the door and go in myself." I laughed. "I won't tell anybody about this."

"About what?" she asked with a whole lot of cross in her voice.

"That you couldn't stop me because of my badge."

"I've seen badges before."

"Sure, all the sheriffs of the last twenty years or so. But they're afraid of the Flannerys, which means they're also afraid of you. But I'm not afraid of either one of you."

"You really won't say anything to anyone?"

"I promise." I smiled at her again. She was part of the town's lore. I didn't want to ruin that lore for her *or* the town.

"You always keep your word, do you?"

"Unless somebody pistol whips me and sets my hair on fire. Then I can't guarantee a thing."

Then the unbelievable happened. Mrs. Milligan smiled. "You're an awfully fresh young man."

"I try to be, Mrs. Milligan. I really try to be. And thanks for saying I'm 'young.' It isn't true but I guess we'll just let it stand."

"The same way we'll let it stand that you won't tell anybody?"

I worked up another smile for her. "Exactly the same way, Mrs. Milligan."

"I figured you'd be in mourning, Flannery."

He had his feet up on his desk—a pair of fine hand-tooled boots he wore—and a magazine hiding his face when Mrs. Milligan rang a bell letting him know somebody was on his way in.

He pulled the magazine down, looked at me and said: "I thought I might see you sooner or later. I was hoping for later."

I sat down. "You could always confess and make everything easier for everybody all around. You being such a public-spirited citizen and all."

He took his feet down, closed the magazine, dropped it on his otherwise clean desk. "What would I be confessing to?"

"You killed Sloane, the first federal man out here."

"Now why would I do that? He was helping try to find Mike Chaney."

"Exactly. You shot him in the back assuming Chaney would get blamed for it."

I glanced around his office. Everything but the man himself was mahogany or rich dark leather.

"But the town didn't get all excited by Sloane dying because they still thought Mike was their hero, even if he had killed him. Nordberg couldn't get enough men for a posse. Nobody wanted to ride on it because they knew there would be hell to pay when they got back to town. Folks didn't want anybody riding after him. And they wouldn't be happy about anybody who did. Then Connelly and Pepper came to town. You tried to get folks all stirred up again by killing Tom Daly. Even if Nordberg couldn't get a posse together, you didn't have to worry. You had Connelly and Pepper ready to go after him. And you made sure they'd go after him and kill him because you sweetened the pot. I don't know how much you gave them but they weren't the kind who worked cheap. Then all you had to do was wait for somebody to bring Chaney's body back. You think your wife would forget him even if he was dead?"

He jabbed a finger at me, arrow true. "You leave my wife off your filthy tongue. She forgot all about Mike Chaney a long time before we even got married."

"You don't really believe that, do you?"

I said it soft, with a hint of pity in the words. It's an old interrogation trick. A soft tone confuses them. They'd expect you to shout something like that, really assault them with it. They weren't sure how to react.

He started to get mad and then he slumped in his chair. "We all think of old lovers. It doesn't mean anything." He waved a hand through the air, dismissing the offending thought. "She probably *did* think of him from time to time. But that doesn't mean she did anything about it. I think of girls I courted before my wife. It doesn't mean anything at all—if you don't do anything about it."

"But you had two reasons to hate him."

"If you mean the banks, we're doing just fine."

"But you don't have the land you wanted for those Eastern investors."

His laugh was unexpected. "That's the trouble with gossip. You can never be sure which part of it is true. I've found some other land for the Eastern folks. And they're giving it a lot of thought."

"Meaning they haven't said yes."

"Meaning they haven't said yes."

He leaned forward again. "I'm willing to make you a substantial bet, Ford."

"I'm not much of a gambler."

"I'm willing to bet you that you don't have any way to connect me to Mike's murder."

"Not yet I don't. But I've just started looking around." He started to speak. I held up my hand. "Where were you yesterday?"

"I went to Bent River."

"What time did you leave?"

"Eight o'clock."

"You take a train?"

"I rode my horse."

"In weather like this?"

"The weather to the east was fine."

"Who did you see in Bent River?"

"I didn't see anybody. I should have said that the weather was fine until I got halfway there. Then it started to snow pretty bad so I turned back for town here."

"Any way of verifying you actually went there?"

A smirk. "You could always ask my horse."

"Did you see anybody on your trip?"

"Not a soul."

"What time did you get back here?"

"About seven o'clock."

"Took you a long time to get back here considering that you only got halfway to Bent River."

"Shoe came loose on my horse."

Now it was my turn to smirk. "You leave town for Bent River. But you have to turn back halfway there. I'm told that's about a three-hour trip. So if you turned back at midpoint that means you should have been back in town here by one o'clock at the latest."

"I told you. A shoe came loose on my horse."

"And it took you all afternoon to fix it?"

He leaned back. "You enjoy this, don't you? You get to come in here and push me around because of that badge of yours. You're not my social equal in any way. You could never get into my clubs; you'd never get invited to any of the parties I go to; you don't have any real standing anywhere—but you've got your badge. And that means that you get to take out all your envy on whoever you want to."

He stood up. "But you know what? I really don't give a damn about your badge. Or about you. Investigate me all you want but you won't be able to prove a damned thing. Because I'm smarter than you. You have the badge but you don't have the brains, Ford." He pointed to the door. "The next time I see you, you'd damned well better have some evidence. Or I'm going to wire some friends of mine in Washington and have you pulled off this investigation. And don't think I can't do it."

I didn't say anything. There was nothing to say. I put my Stetson on and left.

When I came up next to Mrs. Milligan's desk, she said, "Remember your promise."

"It's safe with me, Mrs. Milligan."

She looked relieved.

Chapter 25

You want beans and pipe tobacco, you go to the general store. You want whiskey and gossip, you head for the saloon.

From what I could overhear while I stood at the crowded bar sipping on a root beer, more than a few of the men in town figured that Flannery had killed everybody. They figured what I figured. He had two reasons to do it, just as I'd told Flannery—his wife and his banks. Nobody else seemed to be in the running.

More than a few blamed Flannery's wife. A woman like that, one who couldn't make her mind up, a woman who'd go back and forth between them like that, a woman so selfish she'd put two men through all that anger and humiliation—a woman like that was just as guilty as the man who actually pulled the trigger.

But after a few more drinks, they'd swing back to Flannery. That no-account, no-good, fancy-dressin', spoiled-brat, cold-hearted, thinks-his-shit-don't-stink son of a bitch. Killin' poor Mike Chaney the way he did. Hell with all those federal men what died. It was poor Mike Chaney they mourned. Onliest one with balls enough to rob them banks and give the money back to the people so they could hold on to their little farms and ranches. Nobody else give two turds about them people except poor Mike Chaney. And then a smart-steppin', fancy-pants, lyin'-through-his-teeth bastard hides in some trees and shoots poor Mike in the back. Don't even have guts enough to face him front on. Oh, no, not that silk-underweared chicken-shit ruffled-shirt prick Flannery.

I went to three saloons that night—I take my duties seriously—and in every one of them the palaver was just about the same.

The third saloon, though, was a little more intense because it had a spellbinder leading the uproar.

His name was Nick Tremont. He was one of the men I was supposed to see.

The only time I'd seen him before he was angry but in a controlled, civil way. But that night he was rousing the troops. And he knew how to do it.

He had the kind of strong body, white hair, and thunderous voice that has marked the patriarch of every tribe of men dating all the way back to Old Testament days. He didn't shout the way the preachers did; he didn't exhort the way a lawyer does when he faces a jury. Instead, he spoke quietly, reasonably. And in the smoky bar, lighted only by low-hanging Chesterfield lamps over the tables and two large lanterns behind the bar—the whole room listened patiently and silently as he ticked off reason after reason why somebody else would now have to pick up Mike Chaney's work.

"You know how I hated Chaney. I hold him responsible for killin' my son when he didn't have to; when he killed him only because he wanted to, not because he had to. But I never talked against the job he was doin'. He saved a good part of this valley and there sure ain't any doubt about that."

"What you gettin' at, Nick?" someone asked.

"I think you know what I'm getting at but you're afraid to say it." He stood up tall in his brown leather coat, a Colt on his hip and cold rage in his brown eyes. His gaze took in the men before him, one by one. His lips moved silently as his gaze searched the room. He appeared to be counting.

"I look out here and what do I see? I see four more men who could lose their ranches within the next sixty days. I have it from someone in the bank—a man who won't come forward because he's afraid he'll lose his job, and I can't blame him for that—a man who told me that Flannery has convinced his Eastern money friends to be patient—that he'll have six or maybe even seven spreads for them in the next few months. You men know who you are."

"Ain't one of them spreads yours, Nick?" asked a rancher.

"It sure is. And that's why I say as much as I hated him for killin' my boy, I think he was doin' the right thing where Flannery was concerned."

And then we came to the part that everybody was waiting to hear. A man in the back said: "What're you saying we should do about it, Nick?"

A long pause. His eyes surveyed the room once again. The only sounds were a few coughs and somebody setting down a beer glass.

He said: "I'm not saying anything other than this is somethin' we should think about. Maybe have a little meetin' about."

"You mean right now?"

"Good a time as any, ain't it?"

I doubt there was a man in the saloon who didn't know what was being talked about there. Nobody was going to say anything out loud because if anything actually did happen, he might be blamed for starting it.

"Well, let's get some more whiskey over here and push these tables together and have our little meeting."

The man behind the bar didn't look happy about it. But what could he do? These men were in no mood to be contradicted.

He nodded to my empty glass. I shook my head. There were things I needed to do.

"Well, no sir, not a one of them," the liveryman said.

The wind was up again. It raced through the places where the walls weren't flush and rattled the doors up top. He was an older man with a bad complexion left over from boyhood. He kept his thumbs hooked into his bib overalls whenever possible. He liked to rock on his heels while keeping his thumbs in place. He reminded me of a statue that was about to fall over.

"But there's a reason none of them come in here for their horses."

"Why's that?"

"They keep their own horses. I'd like to have their

business but the only one who gets anything out of 'em is Tully the blacksmith. Now that's the business I shoulda gone into."

It never comes easy. I'd had this daydream that I'd go over to the livery and he'd give me the names of one or two men on the list who rode out at about the right time to meet up with Connelly and Pepper and Mike Chaney. Flannery was still the likely man. But you need to have proof.

"So Tremont and Long don't keep their horses here, either?"

"No, they don't."

So much for my daydream.

"Well, I appreciate it," I said.

As I turned to leave, I saw Nordberg's wife, Wendy, hurrying along the street, the wind pushing her faster than she usually walked. She held her bundled baby wrapped tighter than ever. A number of people joined her in the wind-pushed rush. Men held on to Stetsons and bowlers; women held on to scarves and bonnets. Even the kind that tied under chins got roughed up in weather like that.

I fell into step with Wendy Nordberg and said, "Evening, ma'am."

"Evening, Mr. Ford."

I'd forgotten how fine her features were.

"Would you happen to know where I could find your husband?"

"Probably at the office. Though I can't be sure. With his job he could be anywhere."

We had to raise our voices to hear each other. Whirling snow ghosts danced down the street. The bloody sun sinking then; the first stars appearing.

"In case I don't find him, tell him some men are talking about Flannery, getting all worked up. I don't like the sound of it."

"You mean lynching?"

"I don't want to put any words in their mouths. And since I don't know any of them I don't know how serious they are when they get worked up. Maybe most of them have gone home for supper. But maybe not."

The dying light was such that I couldn't get a good look at her face but I did glimpse her eyes. I'd scared her. I should have thought of what it would be like to hear that your spouse might be facing a lynch mob in an hour or two.

"Tell him I'll meet him at the office at seven. That'll give him two hours for supper. I'll stay down around here and check in at the saloon. Keep an eye on those men."

"I'd really appreciate it, Mr. Ford," she said. "Well, good night."

After she was blown farther down the street, I went to my hotel room. I wrote out a telegram, some of it in code, explaining to the boss that Connelly and Pepper had been murdered and that I was staying in town until I found out who had done it. Then I mentioned Tom Daly and asked if he could contact Tom's wife. I knew it was a chickenshit thing to do and that by rights I should have done it. But she didn't like me much and getting the word from me would only make her more miserable. She liked the boss and he liked her. At the Washington Christmas party the agency always throws, the boss always dances her around the floor a few times. Everybody likes to watch because when you see a stiff old fart like the boss beaming on the likes of a fresh pretty woman, you realize that he really does belong to our species after all.

It took three cigarettes and two drafts to get it down the way I wanted. I hate writing telegrams in a Western Union office. There's a pressure, real or imagined, to hurry. I've got enough pressure on me.

Chapter 26

Once I was back on the street, the first place I checked was the saloon where Tremont was holding his meeting. The men were rowdier by then. Most of them were married and had imbibed right through the supper hour, which was a bad sign. Only the real drunks drink through the supper hour. The barman glanced at me a couple times, inclined his head to the men over in the corner, and then made a face.

Tremont stopped once and turned to me. "This is a private meeting, sir. I ain't tryin' to be rude but I think it'd be best if you went somewhere else to do your drinking."

The men, as one, snarled their approval.

"You don't give the orders in my place," the barman said.

"You be careful, Fred. We can always take our business elsewhere," Tremont said. "And I mean permanent."

I walked over to the men. "I have the authority to arrest every one of you. But I won't if you'll break this meeting up and go home and sleep it off and meet me back here tomorrow morning."

"You can't arrest us," one of the men said. "There's too many of us. You wouldn't stand a chance."

"That's probably true. But I could arrest some of you and then the rest of you would be charged with resisting arrest. Sooner or later you'd be in jail." Several more joined the snarling. It was pretty incoherent. But it was the tone that mattered. They'd let Tremont work them up real nice. Pillaging and sacking would be on the agenda soon enough.

"You're pushing these men into trouble, Tremont. Pretty soon they'll all have guns in their hands and they'll do something stupid. And that might include shooting somebody."

"Like I said, this is a private meeting," Tremont said.

"There's a way to handle Flannery. This isn't the right way. You're drunk and mad and I can understand that. But you sure as hell don't want to do something that you'll be paying for the rest of your lives." I looked around at the hard faces of hard-working men. "You've got families. Think of how they'd feel if Nordberg or I had to ride out and tell them that you're in jail because things got out of hand. And that you're facing prison sentences or maybe even worse. How'd that go over with your wife and kids?"

"He's gonna take our farms!" a man bellered.

"I don't know if that's true and neither do you. But I'm going to ask Flannery about it. I'm going to tell him that he's going to have a lot more trouble if he goes back to foreclosing on his customers the way he has."

"He lies, anyway," Tremont said. "He's tellin' everybody that he's got this other land west of here he's gonna sell those Easterners. But that's bullshit. They wouldn't want that land. Takes damned near an acre to graze two cows. Our land's what he wants. And he's gonna go back to takin' it. We ain't recovered from that drought two years in a row. There's no way we can pay off our farms."

"You didn't let me finish," I said. "This meeting tomorrow—"

"We can't meet tomorrow morning," a man said. "We got to be to work early."

"How about the meeting starts at seven right here?"

A couple men laughed. "You couldn't get Fred out of bed at seven in the morning if you put a rattlesnake in his bed."

I looked back at Fred. "Fred's gonna lend me his keys. I'll open the place up and we'll meet here. One thing—nobody drinks liquor. The meeting'll last an hour and then you can get back to your farms and ranches."

"I still don't see the point of this meeting," Tremont said.

"We're going to have a special guest. Flannery."

"Flannery!" Tremont said. "No way you could get him here—especially at seven o'clock."

"He'll be here."

One man said, "You gonna guarantee that?"

"Yeah. I'm gonna guarantee that. He'll be here and we're all gonna have a meeting. But I want a guarantee from you." I scanned the faces again. "I want you to guarantee me that right after I leave here, you'll all go home and get some food in your bellies and get to bed early so you can be at this meeting in pretty good shape."

They were drunk but not so drunk that they could overlook their families. You get them a little sentimental and they'll back off. My hope was to get them pushing their way through those batwings and on their way home. This wasn't just Tremont. Mobs feed on themselves even if they don't have a leader. Flannery I'd have to worry about later. But he was the best lever I'd been able to use.

"I'm going to help you out, mister," Fred said. He brought up a sawed-off shotgun from behind the bar and said, "I'm closing in five minutes and I don't want no arguments. And if you decide you never want to come back here, fine by me. I'll find other customers. Don't you worry about that." He held his sawed-off tight to his body, ready to fire. "Five minutes. And the federal man here can stick around to watch you go."

A pair of men picked up their coats, shrugged into them and started for the door that covered the batwings.

"You gonna shoot us if we don't go, Fred?"

"I'm sure thinkin' about it."

"I don't like you no more, Fred," one man said.

"Well, I don't like people who talk about lynchin'. Last town I live in, seems like they lynched couple men a month. Sometimes they didn't have no idea whether he was innocent or guilty. They was just pissed so they had to hang somebody."

Tremont said, "Glad you think so highly of us, Fred."

"I did until tonight," Fred said, "until you started talking crazy and all."

They took ten minutes instead of five, the last of them did, anyway. Fred kept his sawed-off on them the whole time.

"Good riddance."

"A few of them probably won't come back."

"I meant what I said. That place I was talkin' about was lynch-happy. And hell, the sheriff there threw in with it. He never even tried to stop 'em." He put the sawed-off down on the bar, lifted up a shot glass and poured himself a full one. "Back in the pioneer days when there wasn't even a judge who rode circuit, sometimes I s'pose they didn't have no choice but to lynch the real bad ones. But nowadays there's no excuse. Got a judge, got a courthouse. No excuse at all."

"No argument here. Thanks for your help."

Chapter 27

Nordberg wasn't in his office but his night man, Dob Willis, was. He sat at the front desk reading a dime novel, a corncob pipe tucked into the left side of his mouth.

"Hey, hi there, Mr. Ford." He was still a kid with cheeks full of freckles and a cowlick as tall as a small tree.

"There might be trouble tonight, Dob."

"Trouble?" he said. And dog-eared his dime novel and set it down. He took the pipe from his mouth. "That don't sound good."

I explained to him what was going on.

"Tremont? Hell, he hated Mike Chaney. Now he wants to go after Flannery himself?"

"Yeah, I thought that was pretty strange, too. But he's got a little bit of preacher in him and you get enough whiskey in those men and some preacher talk about good and evil and all of a sudden you've got yourself a lynch mob."

"Well, the sheriff, he sure don't hold with lynchin'."

"You know where he is?"

"Deliverin' a foal out to the Brammer farm. The doc's busy treatin' a boy that got lost in the storm yesterday. Don't know if he'll make it. Doc usually doubles up as the vet around here. But since he's busy he asked the sheriff. The widow woman Mrs. Gantry, she's all alone on her little acreage near the edge of town. She's got the rheumatism and arthritis too bad to birth a foal. The sheriff usually spells the doc when the doc can't make it."

"Well, I've got some other things to do, so if you see him before I do, tell him to keep an eye on the saloons here. They might just have gone someplace else."

"Well, I'll make them rounds right now. There won't be no lynchin' in this town, I'll tell you that for sure."

"C'mon in but be real quiet. She's asleep."

Jen put a shushing finger to her lips and stood back so I could step in. The wind was such that she had to hold on to the door before it was ripped off its frame.

When I was inside, she tried to help me off with my sheepskin but I said, "I have to get back right away. But I needed to check on something. And I know you'll give me a straight answer."

"Say, I'm impressed. Asking me for my opinion. I must be a lot smarter than I think I am."

The banter was light but the solemn eyes told of her sorrow. Be a long time before the worst of her loss would be over. Her brother had been her best friend and confidant.

She pointed to one of the chairs next to the pot-bellied stove.

"How's Clarice?"

"When she's awake, she's pretty good. But when she's asleep—her nightmares must be terrible. She wakes up about every hour screaming her head off."

"You look good."

"Thanks."

And she did. Her hair was pulled back, she wore a pair of butternuts and a white blouse that flattered a body that didn't need any more flattering, and her eyes were clear from sleep and good food.

"You look pretty keyed up."

"I am. Tremont's got a bunch of the town boys thinking about a lynching."

"Tremont? Who's he want to lynch?"

"Flannery."

"He's going to take over where my brother left off—except up the ante."

"They all seem to think that Flannery's lying about selling some of his western land to his Eastern investors. They think he'll just seize more land when their payments come due."

"That's what he's telling people? That he's going to sell them that land he owns west of here? That's about the poorest grazing land outside of Utah or Montana up in the mountains. Nobody'd buy that land for cattle. Nobody. He's been trying to sell it for years and his father tried before him. You could build a town up there. There's a big timber operation in that area. The way everything's growing, a small town could probably do right nice for itself. But not cattle. No way."

"Well, I figured you'd know if anybody would. I just wanted to check Tremont's facts. I guess he was telling the truth."

Just then Clarice cried out for her mommy. Jen touched my arm and said, "Well, if nothing else, I'd like to cook you a good meal before you leave town. I have to admit, I wanted to blame you for Mike's death—not because you deserved it, but because I needed to blame someone. And I guess I still do. But not you. You tried your best to save him, I know that, and, to be honest, right now you and Clarice are about the only two people in the world I want to see."

I took her to me, hugged her for a long moment. I'd been hoping for more than a meal. She got more attractive to me the more I saw her, and not just physically. She was a damned fine woman in every sense.

Clarice cried again.

"I need to go," she said.

"I know."

This time we kissed briefly and then she hurried into the bedroom.

Chapter 28

I went back to my hotel room to pull on a sweater. Though the wind had died down, the temperature was still in the teens. I had a feeling that I was going to need some heavy clothes before the night was over.

The desk clerk didn't warn me. He was reading a magazine when I came in. He looked up, nodded a greeting and then went back to his reading.

I went up the stairs, dug my key out of my pocket, and started to push it into the lock. That was when I saw that the door was not snug with the frame. I was sure I hadn't left it open.

I pulled my .44 from its holster, pressed myself flat against the wall on the side of the door, and then used my toe on the door to push it open.

A long silence.

Then a female voice: "The only weapon I have, Mr. Ford, is a hat pin."

At first I didn't recognize the voice but then she said: "It's Loretta DeMeer, Mr. Ford. It's safe to come in."

I still didn't take any chances. People weren't supposed to be in your room unless you invited them. Not even very good-looking middle-aged women with only hat pins to protect them.

I stood in the open doorway, my .44 still in my hand.

"You look like a magazine illustration, Mr. Ford. I guess it's the way you're sort of crouched down. And your .44 all ready to shoot."

Quick check of the room. She seemed to be alone. "How'd you get in here?"

"The desk clerk's daughter is in our choir at church. We're old friends."

I holstered my gun and closed the door. She sat on the only chair. I sat on the bed. I reached over and turned up the lamp.

She was as tawny and lush as some great creature of myth, the enormous brown eyes dazzling with amused confidence. She wore a brown seaman's sweater and tan riding pants. The rich abundance of the body and the shining blond hair would be right at home in both an elegant apartment and the jungle. It just depended on where she wanted to eat you up.

"Any particular reason why you're here?"

"Well, a couple of reasons. I should've introduced myself that day at the library for one thing. You looked intelligent. My husband was a book reader. That was one of the many reasons we got along. And one of the reasons I still miss him. And for another reason, I'd like to convince you that I'm not some harlot who seduced Mike Chaney, despite what Jen and the town think."

"Why do you give a damn what I think of you?

Why would you care what people think, Mrs. De-
Meer? You're rich. You've got one of the biggest
spreads in the Territory. I don't even know why you
work at the library."

"I like being around books. And it gets me away
from the ranch. I only work there a few hours a
week. It's a nice break from worrying about cattle
and the price of feed and how many hands short we
are at any given time."

"I still don't know why you care what people
think."

She shrugged and put her head down, seeming
to study the hands that lay in her lap. "I don't de-
serve my reputation." Then she startled me by
starting to cry.

"Mrs. DeMeer, I don't know why you're here but
I'm pretty busy tonight and I'm really not good at
this."

When she raised her head, her eyes were as shiny
as her golden hair. "Not good at what? At listening
to women? Admit it. You think I'm some kind of
whore."

Now I put my own head down, studied my own
hands. This was confusing, her in my room crying.
Confusing and irritating.

"You know how long I was chaste after my husband died?"

I kept my head down. I felt stupid. I didn't know
why she was saying all these things.

"Eight years. I was chaste for eight years. I didn't
so much as kiss another man. But that didn't stop all
the rumors. The women in town were afraid I was
going to steal their husbands. It was ridiculous. I

never flirted with anybody, I never even gave a hint that I was available in any way. But that didn't matter. They still whispered about me, anyway. Do you know what that's like, Mr. Ford? To have people smirk when they see you; and then whisper something when you pass by? To be shunned? Even at church they didn't accept me. They pretended to. But nobody ever invited me for dinner. I was always the outsider and I was ashamed of myself for some reason, even though I wasn't anything like they said I was. Nobody ever invited me to church activities—I had to invite myself. And all that time I was chaste. Completely chaste. Then I took up with Glen, my foreman. And it wasn't this mad passionate affair everybody winked about. His wife and daughter had drowned in a flash flood a few years earlier. He was in as much pain as I was. A lot of the time we didn't even make love. We were just comfortable with each other. Just talked and played cards and sometimes I'd read to him."

"And then you took up with Mike Chaney."

"Not the way you think. He worked on my ranch from time to time. One day I saw him just sitting under a tree with his head in his hand. I went over to talk to him." She smiled. "He couldn't help himself. He flirted with me. He just did it by instinct. I could tell he didn't mean anything by it. It was just the only way he could deal with women. I just ignored it and asked him what was wrong. He wouldn't tell me at first. Then he just opened up. He was like a little boy. Very sad and very confused. Woman problems. This was before he started robbing Flannery's banks. He had two women pregnant and both of them were married and both of them were sure the children were his."

I was rolling a cigarette and she said, "May I have one of those?"

It was still considered scandalous behavior, women smoking cigarettes. But more and more of them were doing it in private. I rolled a good one for her, got it lighted, and carried it over to her.

She took a deep, long drag of it. "Anyway, even when he wasn't working on my ranch, he'd come around just to talk to me."

"About the women?"

"About everything. I think everybody saw him as somebody who never gave much thought to anything. But when you got him alone, he was a lot more serious than that. And I needed a confidant, too. Glen had left—and not because of Mike, despite all the gossip saying otherwise. He'd met a woman at a horse auction over in Drover City about four months ago. He decided right on the spot that he wanted to marry her. She came and visited him once on the ranch and stayed with me overnight. Very nice woman. She and Glen are very happy."

And that was when the gunfire started.

All I could think of was Tremont and his mob.

I went to the window and peered out. In the silver moonlight the shapes of maybe a dozen men could be seen in the middle of the street outside Fred's saloon. That didn't look good.

"Do you have to leave?"

"Afraid I do."

She stood up, came to me. "What I wanted to ask you was if you would talk to Jen and tell her the real story. Because nothing happened between her brother and me other than friendship. She just wouldn't believe it when Mike told her, either. Would you just talk to her?"

"I will," I said, reaching for my sheepskin.

"Promise?"

"Promise," I said. But I was already out the door.

That long night I'd been dreading? I had a sour feeling in my stomach that told me it was just starting.

Chapter 29

Turned out much worse than I expected. Or dreaded, would be more like it.

By the time I reached the dozen or so men in the street, two of the saloons facing that part of the business lane had pretty much emptied. Worth standing in the cold for a show that good.

"You're in big trouble, Jake. Now you let me have that gun back."

There's one thing a lawman probably ought not to do and that's plead with people who are breaking the law. Spit on them, slap them around, kick them in the balls if you get a chance—but don't plead with them.

But poor Dob Willis wasn't experienced enough to know how to handle a situation like that.

I could pretty much figure out what had led to that moment. Young deputy wanting to stay in charge of things hears or sees some kind of commotion down the street. Shrugs into his sheepskin and heads for the spot where all the voices are coming from.

But when he gets there—and this was the part I

wasn't too sure of—somebody or somebodies relieve him of his pistol. And being in a hurry, all excited and everything—being in a hurry, he forgets to grab a carbine from the rack that Nordberg put up for a moment just like that one.

So now he stood in front of the crowd of laughing, jeering, drunken men, begging for them to give him his gun back.

Tremont wasn't the man with Dob's gun but those were the boys he'd stirred up so I walked over to him.

Before he had time to even make a fist, I slapped him hard across the face, grabbed the collar of his jacket, and flung him to his knees right in front of his gang.

"You tell them to give Dob his gun back or I'm going to kick your teeth in."

"You son of a bitch," he said.

"I'm not waitin' long, Tremont. Tell them to give Dob his gun back."

The gallery started shouting.

"It's that federal son of a bitch."

"Hey, federal man, go back to Washington. We don't want you here."

"Kill him, Tremont. Shoot him in the back if you need to."

The man with Dob's gun said, "I ain't givin' him his gun back, Ford. He had to be a big important man and tell us to break it up. Then he made the mistake of wavin' his gun around."

"Give him the gun, Jake," Tremont said, struggling to his feet. And struggling was the right word. Between the liquor and the humiliation of me tossing him around, he wasn't doing well at the moment.

I drew my own .44. "Couple of you boys help him up. And you, Jake, you give Dob his gun back."

Somebody in the gallery shouted, "Hey, Dob, why don't you get your mommy down here? Maybe she can get Jake to give the gun back."

That of course turned out to be just about the most hilarious thing these souses had heard in their lifetimes.

I walked over to Jake. He then had Dob's gun pointed at my chest. "Hand the gun over."

"I could drop you right now." His words were whiskey-wobbly. So was his backbone. He looked ready to fall over, a scrawny man with a rat-mean face.

"Sure you could."

"Better give it to him, Jake," Tremont said.

"Shoot the bastard, Jake," somebody at the back said.

"That's right, Jake," I said. "Shoot me. Waste your whole life on one bullet to impress a bunch of drunks."

Tremont said, "Dammit, Jake. Hand him the gun. Think about your new granddaughter. You want to see her again, don't you?"

Because I was reasonably preoccupied with Jake and the possibility that the drunken yahoo just might kill me, I didn't notice Sheriff Nordberg until he stood to the side of the crowd with his carbine trained right on Jake's temple.

"You got five seconds to hand him the gun, Jake. Or I'll kill you right where you stand."

And that was that.

Nordberg's words managed to penetrate even

Jake's thick head. One glance at the sheriff was all it took. Nordberg was not only big, he was fierce, something I hadn't seen in him till then. I had no doubt he'd kill Jake on the spot. Nobody else did, either, including Jake.

He handed me the gun.

I tried not to look relieved.

"You send these men home now, Tremont," Nordberg said. "And I mean now."

"You throwin' in with Flannery, Sheriff?" Tremont asked.

"If you weren't drunk, you wouldn't even say something like that, Tremont. You know I support you men. But not when you act like this. Now before something bad happens, get these men home. They all have to work in the morning and they'll need a good night's sleep to work off their drunk. Now git and git fast."

"Thanks for helping me with Jake."

"Doing my job is all." He sipped as much coffee as he could. The stuff was scalding. We'd drifted to the café after the men went their various ways home. "Jake's all right when he's sober. He's actually a quiet little fella. But when he gets drunk he thinks he's tough." This time he just blew on his coffee. "And he can be dangerous when he's got a gun in his hand."

"Flannery should think about hiring a bodyguard."

Nordberg smiled. His nose was still red from the night air. "I've told him that, too. He tells me that I should be his bodyguard. Whenever things get kind of threatening, I send a deputy out to stand guard for a shift. It's usually an off-duty deputy, though, so I have to pay him extra, which the town council bitches about."

"Why don't they ask Flannery to pay for the deputy?"

He laughed. "That'll be the day, when that council stands up to anything Flannery wants to do. One of the council members works in Flannery's bank and another one is his second cousin. Flannery gets what he wants and he usually gets it on the cheap. He's a tight bastard."

"I guess that's how the rich get richer." I figured I'd give my coffee a try. It was still pretty hot but I managed to gulp down a taste of it at least. "You have any luck?"

"Went about as expected. Nobody can account for his time yesterday. I'd almost be suspicious if they could. They're out doing chores by themselves or they're checking on their livestock or they take a day trip somewhere. I can check it out if it comes to that. But to be honest, my money's still on Flannery."

"Mine, too."

He yawned. "Be good to get to sleep. In fact—" He pushed his coffee cup away from him. "I better not drink any more of this or I'll be awake all night. A lot of men can sleep on coffee. But I'm not one of them."

He pushed back, picked up his hat, dropped it on his head and said, "Tomorrow morning, I'm going to work on those men again. See if I can't pin them down a little better. There's always a possibility that it wasn't Flannery."

"Maybe we just like him for it because he's such a son of a bitch."

He laughed. "You tryin' to tell me that I don't hand out impartial law and order?"

"Yeah," I said. "I am."

"You know something? You're probably right."

"I got the same problem. I want it to be Flannery, too. You want to see it all catch up to him on the end of a rope."

He feigned mock shock. "Why, you don't understand the ways of the West, mister. Out here the onliest people we hang are poor whites and Mexes and coloreds." The mocking tone vanished. "I don't know about back East but out here a rich man would have to burn down an orphanage before a judge would even consider hanging him."

"It's not any different back East."

"Yeah," he said, standing up. "I kinda figured that."

The wind rattled the window as I tried to sleep. I was in long johns under two blankets and I was still cold. The demons came back, all my drinking years, all the mean and embarrassing things I'd done. Hard to forgive yourself; hard to have any sense of dignity after the whiskey nights come screaming back. I wanted to reach into my head and rip them out so some fine night I could lay my head down and not remember what I'd done and who I was back in those terrible dark days.

I had a nightmare that I was in that room with the wind screeching and distant people screaming and crying as in the aftermath of some disaster. But when

I went to the window the streets were bare. And when I tried the door, it was locked from the outside. The wind got louder and louder and when I woke up—

When I woke up somebody was tapping faintly on my door. My first thought was that it was the wind. But after I sat up and reached for my gun holstered on the bedpost, I heard it again.

Who the hell would be knocking at that time of night?

Chapter 30

Two minutes later I found myself standing in my long johns with my .44 in the face of a tiny gray-haired woman of hunched back and spidery fingers. She had an intensely sweet face, so sweet in fact that I felt stupid holding my gun on her.

"Is that loaded, young man?"

"Yeah, I guess it is."

"Well, you're not going to shoot me, are you?"

"No, I guess not."

"I know this is late."

"Gosh, I guess I hadn't noticed that. Couldn't be any later than one, two o'clock in the morning."

"Now you're making fun of me."

She huddled inside her long draped black coat. The red wool scarf lent her face a touch of vivid color.

"I need to know who you are."

"Mrs. Ralston."

She sounded as if I should have known who that was. I had no idea.

"Tim Ralston. He owns the livery?"

"Oh, I see."

But I didn't. What the hell was the wife of the livery owner doing at my door that time of morning?

"He would've come himself but he's scared. He needs to talk to you. It's important."

"Did he tell you what it's about?"

"He said he just needed to talk to you and it was important. He wouldn't tell me what it was. That's the way he is. He knows all these things about people in town but he won't trust me with anything. He told me somethin' once and I kind've gossiped about it with my friends and it got all over town and he blamed me. The person it was about, he had to move out of town, it got so bad. So Tim won't tell me anything ever since that time."

"So he wants me to come out there now?"

She nodded. "He's scared. Whatever it is, he just wants to get it off his chest. He said you was in and askin' him questions and that he told you a lie and that he's sorry he done that."

A lie.

I'd asked him about two people, Tremont and Long, whose son Flannery had fired after the robbery. I wondered which one he'd been lying about.

"Dress warm," she said. "It ain't far but it's mighty cold."

She waited in the hall while I dressed. Tremont or Long. I still wanted it to be Flannery. No family had the right to "own" a town the way they did that one. It was like the mining towns where the company owned all the stores and the houses the miners lived in. I didn't see much difference between that sort of situation and the socialism that was finding so much support in the workingman ranks.

I dressed warm the way she told me to.

Chapter 31

The Ralston house was a long, narrow adobe structure that sat on the side of a hill and was sur-
rounded by oak trees. A lamp burned in the front
window, sitting on a table and shining in the night
like an icon.

When we reached the front door, Mrs. Ralston
said, "It shouldn't be open."

But it was, not by much, maybe half an inch. The
wind had died down so the door stood still.

I drew my gun. "Let me go in first."

"Oh, Lord, I hope he's all right."

"Wait here, Mrs. Ralston. I'll be right back."

St. Patrick's Cathedral in New York couldn't have
had many more paintings of Jesus than this one did.
Or much more palm from Palm Sunday. Or Bibles
and prayer books lying around. I was a fallen-away
Catholic but all this was familiar to me. My folks
hadn't ever become fanatical about their religion but
whenever I had to stay with my Uncle Norm and
Aunt Bess, this was the environment that damned
near suffocated me. My Aunt Bess knew the names of

every saint in the Book of Saints. She also knew what
ailment/catastrophe/dilemma was confronting you.
Sneeze and she'd tell you the name of the saint who
protected sneezers; open a window and she'd tell you
the name of the patron saint of windows; curse and
she'd tell you the name of a saint who'd gotten his
tongue cut out because he wouldn't deny his religion.
That particular one was supposed to be a moral les-
son for me. Here was this saint who willingly let
them cleave his tongue with a knife—and here I was,
tongue intact, taking the Lord's name in vain.

The whole house was churchlike. Rosaries or palm
were draped over every framed painting of Jesus and
in the bedroom alone I counted three Bibles.

The only thing that interested me was the note that
had been left on the table where they ate their meals.

HONEY SEND THE FEDERAL MAN AWAY.
I'LL BE BACK IN THE MORNING.

I called out Mrs. Ralston's name. She came inside
breathing hard, wound tight from the mystery of the
situation.

I handed her the note.

"Oh, good Lord," she said, crossing herself. "He
must be in some kind of trouble. Maybe whatever he
was going to talk to you about. Do you think somebody came here and took him away?"

"I don't think so. I can't be sure. But look around.
The place isn't messed up. And I happened to notice
that there weren't any footprints in the snow when
we came up here. Is there a back door?"

She nodded. Led me to a large enclosure that

served as a washroom and a pantry. A door was at its end.

I opened the door, looked out. "Hold your foot up, would you?"

I got a good impression of the size of it and then stepped out on the small stoop. In the moonlight I could see two sets of footprints. One of them was hers. And one of them had to be her husband's. Had to be because there were no other prints to see.

"Doesn't look like anybody took him away."

"He was nervous about talking to you, that was for sure."

"Any idea where he might have gone?"

For the first time her small, elderly face showed cunning. She was one of those virtuous people who couldn't lie well.

"Nearly anywhere. He knows a lot of places he could go."

"You sure about that?" I forced her to meet my eyes.

She gulped before she lied. "Yeah. Like I said, he knows a lot of places."

I knew she wasn't going to help me. She'd caught her husband's fear.

"Well, maybe you can give him a message for me. A lot of people are awfully upset right now. There was some ugly talk yesterday, and it'll only get worse if he doesn't agree to meet with the townfolk. I've set something up for tomorrow morning. You know where I'm staying. He should meet me at sunup. He can find me in my room or having breakfast at the Star Café."

"They have good flapjacks, don't they? That's our

treat. Every once in a while we go to the Star and have flapjacks. They've got that maple syrup there. That's what my husband likes. That maple syrup."

She was babbling. I got her out of her misery. "Well, I need to be going now. Still got a few hours sleep before dawn."

"I'm sorry I had to wake you up—and for nothing, it turned out."

"That's all right. Just remember to tell him where he can find me."

She followed me through the house to the front door.

"I'll be sure to tell him soon as I see him."

I opened the door on a freezing winter night. Even though the wind was down, the cold cut through me.

When I had been out on the back stoop, I had taken notice of where the footsteps led. There was a barn down the street from them. When I left the house I walked the length of what looked to be their property. The footsteps came all the way to the street. They were lost briefly on the narrow road, then they picked up again in the snow leading to the barn.

I figured he was probably up in the haymow watching me. I had to make it look good. I walked down the street. The barn was the property of McGraw's Seed Company. That's what the sign said anyway.

I walked past the barn, far enough that he would have given up watching me. I was pretty sure he assumed I had just kept going straight back to my hotel, which was only about three blocks away.

But I tramped over to the railroad tracks and walked on ties all the way back to the barn. I came down into a gully where I sank into snow that was up to my hips.

He made it easy for me.

He'd left the back door half open so I could slip inside without making any noise. And as I stood in the deep cold shadows of the ground floor, he did me the favor of coming down the ladder from the mow.

The one problem I had was fighting my allergies. The interior of the place was three-quarters filled with bags of seed. My eyes started to run and my sinuses reared up with one of those sneezes that could knock a wall down.

But somehow I managed to fight the sneeze back down.

I pulled out my .44 and walked over to the ladder just as his left foot touched the ground.

"Need to talk to you, Tim."

He screamed. He fell back into the ladder, nearly knocking it down, putting a hand over his heart.

"Shit, you scared the hell out of me."

This time when the sneeze came up I let it go full blast. I thought the damned barn was going to collapse all around us, the way that sneeze exploded on dark air.

"Sinuses?" he asked.

"Yeah."

"The missus can't even come in this place without she's plugged up for three, four days afterward. She's tried every kind of patent medicine she can find."

"None of them work." I sneezed again.

"You're just as bad as the missus."

"How about we go back to your house and have some coffee?"

"I'm not going to tell you nothing."

"We'll see."

"No, we won't see. You're a federal man. You get to ride out of here when it's all over. Me, I got to live here. I've had that livery business for going on twenty years. I'm too old to move and too old to start any other kind of business. Plus, I love horses. I couldn't work in no store or nothing. I'd miss the horses too much."

"A lot of people have died. I need to find out what's going on. Now let's go back to your place. It's cold as hell in here."

"I tell you, it won't do you no good. I thought about it and I just can't afford to get involved."

"You know who killed Mike Chaney and the two federal men."

"I don't know any such thing and if the missus said otherwise, she's wrong. All I know is the names of a couple people I forgot to mention to you. That don't mean they had anything to do with the killing. And if I sic you on them, they'll know who told you—and then they'll shun me. That's how they do it in this town. They shun you and they force you out. I'm too old for that. And, anyways, like I said, I'm sure they didn't have nothin' to do with the killing, anyway."

I sneezed again. Son of a bitch. Freezing my balls off and sneezing.

"So there ain't no need for you to come back to the house. I was stupid to have the missus go get you and I sincerely apologize for that, mister. But I changed my mind and no matter what you say to me or do to me, I ain't changin' it back."

Another sneeze.

All this—missing sleep, freezing, a sinus explosion—for not one damned scrap of information.

And I knew he was the kind of old boy who would do just what he said. He wasn't going to tell me anything.

About every thirty feet, all the way back to my hotel, I sneezed.

Chapter 32

In the morning, the temperature soared to twenty-three degrees above zero. Given the way we'd talked about pancakes, all I could think of when I was washing up and shaving was the café's famous flapjacks.

The lobby was busier than usual at six-thirty in the morning. Three or four groups of men stood talking with great urgency. I wondered what the hell could be so important. But even more, I wondered how many flapjacks I was going to order. It would probably be embarrassing to order sixteen of them.

There were knots of people up and down the main street talking with the same kind of urgency as the men in the hotel lobby. Something was going on. I would need to fortify myself with flapjacks before I could hear the news.

The café was elbow-to-belly with people. A thundercloud of tobacco smoke hung at about shoulder level. The women who ran the place looked frantic. The men standing up were waiting for the sitters occupying the counter stools and the tables to de-occupy them.

I didn't give a damn about sitting down. I managed to snag a serving woman and told her that I'd take a stack of six and eat them standing up.

"Really?" she asked, shouting above all the other shouts.

"Really. I'm hungry."

She glanced around and then turned back to me. "You c'mon back with me, if you're that hungry." She leaned closer so that nobody else would hear. I could barely hear. "You can eat in the kitchen."

Walking into the kitchen, which was the size of a large closet, was similar to walking into a steam bath with all your clothes on. "We don't use this stove back here unless it's an emergency—like this morning." She wiped her brow with the back of a pink hand. "Fred, you fix him up with six flapjacks, all right?"

Despite the cold outside, the man standing over the stove with a huge griddle sitting on top of it wore only an undershirt. It was that hot back there. Too hot.

"Tell you what, how about I stand out back and have a cigarette?"

He didn't even look at me. He was busy flipping flapjacks. "Don't make no never mind to me."

"Then I'll come back for my flapjacks."

I went out the back door. I was so hot from the café kitchen that I didn't feel the cold for a couple minutes. The day was one of sunlight and pure white hills of snow. I got a cigarette going and just studied the landscape, the nearby field that stretched into the foothills.

From my right came two men tramping through knee-high snow. They were walking over from the rear door of the wagon works down the block.

As they got near enough to hear, one said to the other, "Oh, he was behind it all right. Man don't kill himself if he's innocent."

They came up to the back door, nodding when they saw me.

I said, "What's all the commotion this morning?"

One was a stocky dark-haired man, the other a stocky bald man with sandy-colored fringes over both ears. Neither wore coats, just work shirts with long johns showing under their shirt cuffs.

"You that federal man?" the bald one asked.

"I am."

"Yeah. Thought so. My little boy's teacher was explaining at school the other day what a federal man does. Now my boy says he wants to be a federal man."

"That's better than mine," the dark-haired man laughed. "He wants to be a bank robber."

His friend smiled. "I'd sure keep an eye on him."

"So what's all the hubbub about?"

"Surprised you haven't heard by now. You know Flannery, the banker?" the bald one asked.

"Sure."

"Blew his brains out last night," the dark-haired one said. "But the way I hear it they didn't find him till about an hour ago."

I jammed my hand into my pocket for some coins. "Would you pay my bill for me? I need to get out to

Flannery's place." I handed the bald one the money. "I appreciate this."

The dark-haired one said, "Glad to help, mister."

Suddenly I'd lost my appetite. Not even those locally famous flapjacks sounded good anymore. I'd planned on a meeting with Flannery that morning, but I'd expected him to be alive for it.

Chapter 33

There were four buggies, three horses, and a sleigh in front of Flannery's mansion.

It was too cold to stand outside for long, so instead of lining up in the street, the neighbors just looked out their windows.

I went straight to the front door. Any other time I would have spent a few minutes studying the massive door and its intricate carvings. But then all I did was knock. A maid, her eyes so puffy and red from crying that they resembled wounds, stood back. I had my badge ready.

"It's so terrible," she said, sniffling. She was a big, sturdy blond woman, unmistakably Swedish. She wore a maid's gray uniform with a white full-length apron over it.

"I'm assuming Sheriff Nordberg is here."

"Yes, he is."

"Please take me to him."

"Sure." She sniffled again, producing a dainty white handkerchief that was turning green. She put it to a tear-raw nose. "He was such a nice, decent man."

The preacher who buried him would say the same thing. By the time the first sob exploded in the church, Flannery would already have been forgiven for all his considerable transgressions. All that remained would be the idealized portrait most of us get at our funerals. Behind closed doors following the funeral—that would be another matter. Then the real feelings, drawn like daggers, would stab the solemn air.

The maid led me down a long hall. The hardwood floor had been polished to diamond brilliance.

A study that six people could live in. One vast wall filled with books. A hardwood floor covered with Persian rugs, real Persian, not Sears and Roebuck Persian. A dry bar. A leather couch angled in front of a fireplace a short man could stand in.

And a desk with a surface size of a tennis court. But the fine-honed craftsmanship of the enormous desk was diminished somewhat by the man lying face down on it, a .38 near his right hand, a lurid pool of darkening blood dripping off the front edge of the desk, and splattering on the Persian rug below.

The doc and Nordberg stood in the west corner, talking.

Nordberg waved me over.

"Glad you came, Noah," he said. "I didn't want him moved until you got here. I sent a deputy for you but apparently you came on your own."

"Just as I was about to eat pancakes."

"At the Star Café?" the doc asked.

I nodded.

"They're something, aren't they?" the doc said. "I get hungry just thinking about them."

"How about you look it over?" Nordberg asked. "You've probably seen a few more suicide scenes than I have."

I shrugged. "Probably not many more. But sure, I'll look it over."

I spent ten minutes at it. I wondered why he wanted me to look it over. There was powder residue on the right temple and that was in line with a man putting a gun to his head and pulling the trigger. The .38 was probably a little farther away from the hand than I would have expected, but one thing about suicides—they usually look a bit funny one way or another. The head is at an odd angle or the wound doesn't seem right for a bullet fired at such close range or—and this is the most common in my experience— the weapon is closer to the body or farther from the body than you would have thought possible.

But given my limited experience with situations like this, nothing seemed wrong in any particular way. No telling what will happen in the seconds following a man slumping over his desk when the bullet has ended his life.

I walked back to Nordberg and the doc. There was something about that huge room that put me in mind of being in church. I realized that we were all talking in lower voices than usual and that nobody had sworn.

"I guess I don't see anything that bothers me," I said.

The doc smiled, his wrinkled face almost simian when he flashed his false teeth. "I know a certain lawman who owes me five dollars."

"You think there's something wrong here?" I said to Nordberg.

He stared at the desk and the dead man. "The gun."

"What about it?"

"It's pretty far from the hand. Maybe two feet."

"Could've slammed down against the desk and then skidded."

"Watch out for the sheriff here when he gets an idea," the doc smiled.

"First of all," Nordberg said, "why would he kill himself?"

The doc said it before I could. "Because he killed those federal men so it would reflect bad on Mike Chaney. Then he rode out there and killed Mike and Connelly and Pepper, though killin' those last two wasn't no crime—not in my book, anyway."

I said, "That's about how I see it."

"He just wasn't the kind to kill himself." Nordberg did some more staring. "Too selfish. And besides, he didn't have any reason to be scared. If he needed an alibi for yesterday, he could've paid somebody for one. But he didn't have an alibi and that's what made me believe that he was probably telling the truth."

"Yeah, but it would all have caught up with him in the end. You can't kill as many people as he did without getting caught eventually." The doc leaned down and picked up his bag. "You have one of your boys drop him off at the funeral home and I'll get an autopsy out for you this afternoon."

"That's a fast autopsy."

"Well," the doc said wryly—and for a while there

I'd forgotten that he owned the funeral parlor as well as having the only doctor's office in town—"since he shot himself in the temple, I don't expect this'll be a real complicated autopsy, Mr. Ford."

And he winked at Nordberg. They probably both had a good time when the federal man got sarcastically upbraided.

"Unless you saw a stab wound I didn't happen to notice," the doc said.

"Just that ax in the back of his head," I said.

He put on his derby. "Now I'm gonna go have some of them flapjacks you were talkin' about. Can't get 'em out of my head. Just like Nordberg here can't get it out of his head that there's something wrong with the situation here."

After he left, Nordberg said, "I went to Denver for a two-week law enforcement program. And I learned one thing."

"What's that?"

He smiled. "Doc doesn't know squat about autopsies."

"I kinda had that feeling."

He took a few steps toward the desk and the dead man. "So you don't see anything wrong?"

"Afraid I don't."

"Maybe it's just this feeling I have. I mean, maybe nothing *looks* wrong but it just—feels wrong. I don't know any other way to say it."

"I guess I see it the way the doc does. It was all coming down on Flannery. I've seen it happen quite a few times. People kill in a kind of frenzy. And sometimes that frenzy can last for quite a while. Weeks, maybe. But then something happens and they realize

what they've done. And it doesn't matter even if they
think they can get away with it. They just can't face
what they've done. And so they kill themselves."

"I guess that's where my doubts stem from. Flannery was a pretty ruthless character. Him feeling so
guilty that he had to kill himself—that's quite a
stretch. For me, anyway."

One of the double doors opened and Laura Flannery
came through. There was nothing vivid about her
now. Her regal bearing had given way to slumped
shoulders and dead dark eyes. She wore a robe she
had spilled something on. Either she hadn't noticed
or didn't care.

"I'm really not up to this, Mr. Ford."

"I'm afraid we have to talk. Not for long. But for
at least a few minutes." She walked over to the desk
where her husband lay dead. She lay her hand on his
shoulder and then closed her eyes tight, as if she was
in some sort of spiritual communication with him.
Then she extended her left arm to the gun on the
desk. She apparently knew enough not to touch it.
"That was a gun I bought him in Chicago. He didn't
like to carry large guns because they ruined the lines
of his suit. He only dealt with the upper classes when
he traveled, of course, and he didn't want to look
like—well, no offense, but he didn't want to look like
some dime-novel thug. So I bought him that. It was
easy to hide and wouldn't spoil the lines of his suit.
He took it everywhere when he traveled."

She looked up at Nordberg. "I bought him that

hunting rifle the same day. The one with the silver inlay? He always took it with him when you went duck hunting, remember?"

I liked her slightly more than I wanted to. She was one of those women rich men buy to reward themselves for their success. But now that was gone. She was just a woman grieving and I had to respect that.

"What was his mood last night?" I asked gently.

She didn't seem to hear me—her hand was still on his shoulder—and then she looked up and said, "Fine. He was even making a few of his terrible jokes." She smiled sentimentally at the memory. "I didn't have the sense that anything was wrong at all."

"Had you had visitors?"

"No."

"Do you remember anything that might have upset him during the day?"

"If there was, he didn't mention it."

"Was his mood generally good the past week or so?"

She raised her head and looked directly at me. "Mike Chaney. Mike Chaney was stealing my husband's money and humiliating him. I hold Chaney responsible for my husband's suicide. I really do."

She put her head down and began choking on her sobs.

"I won't bother you any more, Mrs. Flannery. Thank you. I'll leave now."

"I'll walk you to the door," Nordberg said. "I'll be right back, Laura."

"Goodbye, Mrs. Flannery," I said. "I'm sorry your husband is dead."

We were at the door. The sunlight off the snow was blinding when we got to the porch. The crowd had thinned; most of the vehicles had gone. The sun still shone, the kids still made snowmen, and moms still made hot apple cider for when the mister came in for the noon meal. The world was still the world, even without the important presence of one man named Flannery.

"I'm still not sure it was a suicide."

"Somebody would've had to sneak in and knock him out and then kill him. With all the servants around, that wouldn't be easy."

"What if it was somebody already in the house?"

"Well, in my report it goes down as a suicide. Unless you can come up with something that changes my mind."

"How about stoppin' by the funeral parlor for me?"

"Sure. You want me to give Doc a message?"

"Yeah," he said. "Tell him when he gets the body to look for a knot on his head. Something that would show he'd been knocked out. I didn't see any but it might be a small one."

"You don't give up, do you?"

He said, "Not when I know I'm right."

Chapter 34

The first place I stopped was the livery. I was surprised to find Tim Ralston there. He was in back, talking to a man about boarding his horse. He didn't look happy to see me. Or maybe it was just that the large black circle around his right eye was still painful. Somebody had given him a damned impressive black eye.

"Well, that sounds reasonable," the customer was saying. "I should be back on Tuesday. The wife just doesn't want to be responsible for the old fella. She knows how much I care about him. She's afraid he'll die or somethin' while I'm gone and then I'll blame her." He spat a stream of tobacco juice at a stack of hay bales. "And the thing is, I probably would. So it's better that I leave him here." The customer gave Ralston a cold grin. "Of course, if he'd happen to die while he was boarded here, then I'd blame you." He wasn't kidding and Ralston obviously knew he wasn't kidding. If I hadn't been there to distract him, I imagined Ralston would have told the customer what he could do with his horse. If it would fit.

After the customer counted out some paper money and put it in the left hand of Ralston, he walked away, taking the alley route. Leaving Ralston to look at me and then look as if he was thinking of running away.

"We're going to have a talk, Ralston, whether you want to or not."

The black eye must have still hurt quite a bit. He touched it tenderly. Winced.

"I doubt your wife gave you that."

"Why the hell you have to keep picking on me?"

"Because you made the mistake of sending your wife for me. But then you got scared. It's a pretty good bet that whoever scared you also gave you that black eye."

Behind me a voice said, "Came to get my horse, Tim."

The voice was familiar but I couldn't put a face to it. But I didn't have to. Tremont came up next to me.

"You bet," Ralston said.

He'd found another excuse not to talk to me. Tremont obviously got a good look at Ralston's black eye but didn't say anything about it. Which I thought was pretty damned strange.

Ralston went to get Tremont's horse. And then I remembered something that Ralston had told me the other day. That people like Tremont had no need for a livery. They kept their horses at home on their ranches and farms.

Tremont lit a small cigar and said, "Got kinda rough on the street last night. Guess I had too much to drink."

"Yeah, I guess you did."

"But I guess our problem was taken care of."

"Which problem would that be?"

He smirked. "The Flannery problem."

He wore a black and red checkered winter jacket and he clapped his gloved hands together. It was colder in there than outside, which didn't make a lot of sense.

"You really believe that, Tremont?"

"Yeah. Old man Flannery won't be foreclosing now. He won't have the stomach for it. His son got some of the land he wanted but he had a miserable life doing it."

I said, "You sleep through the night, did you?"

"Meaning what?"

Without realizing it at first, I was slipping into Sheriff Nordberg's notion that Flannery's life hadn't ended by suicide. It had ended by murder.

"Meaning can you prove you went home after the dustup in the street—and stayed there till this morning?"

"My wife'll tell you that I did."

"Anybody else? You got any ranch hands?"

"One. But he was over to the bawdyhouse. He was probably so drunk when he got to the cabin he stays in he wouldn't have no idea if I was there. And what's the difference? Flannery committed suicide."

"Maybe."

"Maybe? What the hell's that mean?"

"The sheriff thinks he was murdered and it was made to look like a suicide."

"Well, that's a crock of shit if I ever heard one." Then he gaped around. "Where the hell's Tim?"

"How come you're boarding a horse here?"

"It's not mine. It's my neighbor's. He's laid up with the shingles. I told him I'd get his horse shoed and pick up some hay for him. I brought my wagon here." Then, "Where the hell is he? I want to get to the café and have some breakfast. I purposely didn't eat this morning. Figured I'd get some flapjacks at the Star. Didn't tell the missus, though. She's sensitive about her cooking. She'd accuse me of not liking her food if she found out I went to the Star for breakfast." Then, cupping his hand to his mouth, "Tim, where the hell are you?"

There was a smaller barn behind the one we were in. I assumed that was where the horses were boarded.

Tremont started walking toward the back door, toward the smaller barn. I was getting curious about Ralston myself.

Tremont went outside, stood there searching for Ralston. "He must still be in the boarding barn."

I went outside and headed for the smaller barn. I guess I already knew what we'd find.

Half the stalls were empty. The place needed a good cleaning. The acid stench of horse shit made me start sneezing. The place was small enough that I could see after a quick walk-through that Ralston wasn't there.

"Hell, here's my neighbor's horse," Tremont said. "But where the hell's Tim? He's supposed to be getting this one ready to go."

"He's gone."

"Yeah, but where?"

"Anywhere I'm not." Then: "You give him that black eye?"

"What black eye?"

"The one that takes up about a third of his face on the left side."

He shook his head miserably. "I got the whiskey flu. Hangover. I didn't even notice no black eye."

If he was telling the truth—and I wasn't sure he was—he must have been suffering a damned bad hangover. That shiner of Ralston's was hard to miss.

"If I see Tim, want me to tell him to look you up?"

"Don't bother," I said. "He wouldn't do it, anyway."

Chapter 35

Half an hour later, I stood on the front steps of the Flannery mansion. Sheriff Nordberg's theory had started to make some sense to me. There wasn't any evidence to point to murder but I thought of what a greedy and ruthless bastard Flannery had been. Nordberg was probably right. Flannery didn't seem like the suicidal kind. He'd kill but it would be somebody else.

You could see all the vehicle tracks in the snow. But everybody had gone home. There was a certain loneliness on the air. As if a big noisy circus had just left town. People weren't even staring out their windows.

The maid answered the door. "She's upstairs asleep. The doc, he give her two big pills."

"I just want to look around. And ask you to look around with me, Mrs.—I didn't catch your name before."

The big blond woman looked stricken. "Mrs. Swenson. I'm not in no trouble, am I?"

"No. Not at all. I just need to know a couple of things."

"It was Whitey, he was the one who stole the silverware and tried to sell it. Like I told the missus, I didn't have notink to do with it."

"I'm sure you didn't. So how about letting me in?"

"You sure I ain't in trouble?"

"None at all."

Two staircases, another fireplace you could fill up with short people, and a ballroom that could probably hold twenty couples on the polished floor. There was even a stand for a three- or four-piece musical group. Heavy wine-colored drapes covered the long windows.

"They use this room much?"

"Not so's I know. He don't like her friends and she don't like his friends. So they just never invited nobody."

"Well, that's one way to settle it."

"It's a shame, beautiful room like that going to waste."

Then we were in the kitchen. With two stoves and half a dozen ice boxes to keep meat and vegetables cold, with maybe as many as thirty pans and pots hanging from a grid suspended from the ceiling. Everything, including all three sinks, shone radiantly in the sunlight through the windows. The view of the mountains from there was stunning. I saw the trail we'd taken looking for Mike Chaney. That seemed like a long time ago. I wondered how Jen and Clarice were doing.

"Where's the back door?"

She led me through a dark back porch that had no windows. It resembled a loading dock for a general store. There were maybe two hundred boxes of various kinds stacked up back there. I couldn't see well enough to figure out if they were stacked in any sort of order but it was hard to imagine they weren't.

"Flannery liked to stock up?" I asked.

"He always said we should have enough provisions to live on for three months in case of some kind of disaster."

"He ever say what kind of disaster he was afraid of?"

"I think earthquakes, but he never talked much to the help."

When we reached the door, she slid back a bolt lock. And swung the door open.

"That's all he had to secure the back door with?"

For the first time, she smiled. It made her round face pretty. "Oh, no. This was what he used to keep out intruders."

As soon as she put one foot down on the back steps, a thunderous eruption blasted the sunny silence. Dogs. Their deep, crazed voices made the universe tremble.

"Take a peek at them, Mr. Ford."

Dobermans. Four of them. They were on long chains that were tethered to a six-foot metal pole. A structure half the size of a good boulder was where they ate and slept. The chains were so long that they didn't have any trouble reaching it. They wouldn't have any trouble with intruders, either. They could rip out a throat in record time.

"Is this always kept locked?"

"Oh, yes. If Mr. Flannery ever found it unlocked, he'd fire you. He and the missus were about the only ones who ever used this back door."

So much for that theory. Nobody had snuck into

the house the previous night to kill Flannery. They wouldn't have been able to get in. Not through the back door, anyway.

"Is there a fire escape?"

"No."

"How about the front door? How is that secured?"

"Three bolt locks."

"Why so many?"

"Well, when he started doing them foreclosures—"

"He got scared?"

She nodded.

"I don't blame him," I said.

"I didn't hold with them foreclosures. Them poor people."

"You ever say anything to Mr. Flannery?"

"Mister, my husband and me got two kids to feed. I need this job bad. If I'da said anything to the mister, he would have kicked me out right on the spot. You ever see his temper?"

"Couple times. How about a cellar? Can you get into it from outside?"

"Sure. There's those tornado doors on the side."

I'd never heard them called tornado doors before, the slanted door or doors that led you down to the cellar from the outside. Usually they were called storm cellar doors.

"Would you show me down there?"

"Sure."

We went back to the kitchen and then to the room adjacent to the back porch. A pine door I'd walked by previously now opened to let us down a flight of stairs to a cellar that smelled harshly of cold air and stone.

The cellar was as well organized as the back porch. Well-constructed shelves held everything from laundry soap to dozens and dozens of jars of jams, jellies, and vegetables that somebody had put up in late summer or early fall. There were two windows on the north side. Dusty sunlight angled through them, a cat lying lazy in one of the golden bars of sunbeams.

"Napoleon, you go on and get upstairs." To me: "He loves it down here."

Napoleon raised his wide head with baronial splendor, taking us in with great disdain, and then got up and left, making it clear that he did not care to spend any time with humans.

On the west side of the house I saw five steps leading to the underside of the slanted storm cellar doors.

"Are the doors locked from outside?"

"No. Mr. Flannery always says that nobody could get past the dogs."

"And nobody ever has?"

"Not that I ever heard of, that's for sure."

"They ever give you any trouble?"

"They snap at me sometimes when I'm hanging up the wash on the clothesline."

"But they leave you alone?"

"Mrs. Flannery taught me their command words. They won't attack you if you yell those words at them loud enough. Otherwise not even the Flannerys could control them. They had some man from Denver come out here and train these dogs. But God help you if you don't know the words."

"How many people know the command words?"

"Not many that I know of."

I walked over to the storm cellar doors. "I'm going to try them on the dogs myself."

"Oh, no! They could kill you."

"You said that you can control them. Then I should be able to, too."

"But you don't know the words."

"I will if you tell them to me."

"Oh, I'm under strict instructions not to—"

"I'm a lawman. Your employer has just died. These are pretty special circumstances, Mrs. Swenson."

To make my point I started walking up the steps leading to the door. "I'm going out there, Mrs. Swenson. With or without the command words."

She didn't have much choice. "Abraham Lincoln's hat."

"Those are the words?"

She nodded. "But I'd still be careful."

I drew my .44. "You don't have to worry about that."

In the war you'd run into dogs sometimes. The worst were the dogs trained to track soldiers. They were relentless. But they weren't killers. The dogs up top had every scrap of normal dog bred and trained out of them. They had only one purpose other than eating and going to the toilet. They killed people. Or they wanted to, anyway. I could see the usefulness of dogs like those but for all their ferocity I felt sorry for them. They enjoyed few if any of the pleasures of being a dog. They were slaves in every sense.

But that didn't keep me from being wary. Or, to put it another way, scared shitless.

I pushed the door back and stood on the second

step looking up at pure blue sky and radiant sunlight. My enjoyment lasted about three seconds.

The dogs made their moves almost instantly. They smelled me, they saw me, they had no idea who I was. In dog lingo the word *enemy* had to be huge in their brains.

Their speed, even in deep snow, was astounding. They had been maybe ten yards from me and then they were maybe three yards from me. Suddenly I realized that they could tear my throat out even though I had a gun. I might be able to kill one of them. But then the other three would make quick work of me.

I shouted, "Abraham Lincoln's hat."

I felt kind of silly, even though the dogs were nearly on top of me by then. What kind of adult wants to be caught shouting "Abraham Lincoln's hat"? It sounded like a line from a little kid's nursery song.

But it worked.

They were still flinging long strings of spittle; their eyes were still trying to fly out of their sockets; their teeth were still gleaming inside their long mouths.

And I had to say it a couple times for them to get the message. But they stopped.

They continued to growl, they continued to strain forward, they continued to eye me with a hatred that would have given pause to Attila the Hun.

But they stopped.

"Are you all right up there, Mr. Federal Man?" Mrs. Swenson shouted from the shadows in the basement below.

"I will be when I quit shaking."

It sounded like a joke but it wasn't. Not only was

I shaking, I was sheened with sweat over my entire body. I hadn't noticed either of those things until just that moment.

I was happy to walk backward down the steps, closing the slanted door after me.

"I said a prayer for you."

"I appreciate that, Mrs. Swenson."

"You see why I'm afraid to hang wash."

"Yeah, I have a pretty good idea."

"All the time I'm out there with the wash I'm worried that they won't obey me even when I shout the command words to them."

"That sort of crossed my mind, too." Only now did I shove my .44 back into its holster.

We went upstairs. From one of the kitchen windows I could see the dogs. They still hadn't settled in completely. They had been deprived of the only pleasure they knew now that they weren't really dogs anymore.

"Thanks very much, Mrs. Swenson. I appreciate all your help."

"You know, I have nightmares about them dogs sometimes."

I smiled. "Yeah, I just might have a few nightmares about them, too."

Even when I went out the front door, I could hear the Dobermans barking out back. They knew everything that went on outside the mansion. I wondered what they knew about what had happened the night before.

Chapter 36

I tried the livery and then I tried Tim Ralston's house. He wasn't at either place.

I was walking back to my hotel when I saw Sheriff Nordberg's wife, Wendy. As always, she had the baby in tow. Not that I could see the child. She had vanished beneath about six pounds of baby blankets.

I tipped my hat and said, "You must be pretty tired by the end of the day."

She smiled. "They say it gets easier." She dug down in the covers and gave the poor little thing some air. "I have to take her to the doc's place. She's got another ear infection. The thing is, she's not much of a crier. That's nice at night but it doesn't tell you much when she's sick." She beamed down upon the face I couldn't see from where I stood. "She's such a good little girl, aren't you, dear one?"

I probably wouldn't make a good father. Just listening to baby talk embarrasses me. Having to speak it would be even worse.

She covered up the child and said, "Well, I'd better get her out of this cold air."

She had one of those faces I wanted to kiss. To tilt up to my face and kiss gently and work my way into the passion. There was a simplicity, a vulnerability to her looks that made me both protective and lustful at the same time.

"Good to see you, Mrs. Nordberg."

"And good to see you, Mr. Ford."

The way she blushed made her even more fetching.

A few minutes later, I was sliding my key into the lock of my hotel room door.

And one minute after that, I found Tim Ralston. He lay on his back on my bed. He'd emptied his bowels at the moment of death so the room wouldn't be one I'd be sleeping in later that night. Oh, no, the hotel folks would be moving Noah Joseph Ford to another room, preferably at the far end of the hall.

A common kitchen knife protruded from his right eye socket. The mix of blood and tissue and eyeball had the texture of suet. But he had been stabbed just before in the chest, near the heart. The killer had wanted to make sure Ralston was dead. Or maybe it was more perverse than that. Maybe he'd stabbed him in the eye for simple pleasure.

I walked to the head of the stairs and shouted down for a bellboy. My voice was loud and rude on the quiet late-morning air.

I heard the desk clerk pound on his bell; moments later I heard somebody taking the steps two at a time and then half-running down the hall.

"Oh, shit," the big raw red-haired kid said when he reached my doorstep. He was probably about fifteen. They'd found him a bellboy's uniform. It was about two sizes too small.

"Right in the fuckin' eye," he said.

"Yeah."

"That poor little bastard."

"You know him?"

"Me'n my brother used to sit on a roof behind his livery and throw rocks at the horses. He got pretty mad at us."

"Just for throwing rocks at his horses? He sure must have been a hothead."

He caught my sarcasm. "Well, that was when I was younger. I'm grown up now." I was still glaring at him. "It was a pretty shitty thing to do."

"Yeah," I said, "I bet the horses liked it even less than Ralston did." Then: "I want you to go get the sheriff and then go to the funeral home and tell them we need their wagon."

He sniffed the air like a pointer dog. "He crap himself?"

"Yeah."

"People do that when they die?"

"Sometimes."

He shook his head. "I sure wouldn't want to be around dead people much. I sure wouldn't want *your* job."

"Sometimes I don't want it, either. Now get going."

I decided I didn't much like the smell, either. I went down to the end of the hall and opened the door and stood on the rickety wooden fire escape. Someday hotel owners would figure out that a fire would burn the wooden escape just as fast as it would the rest of the structure. The better city hotels all had metal fire escapes by then.

The air was good and clean. It was cold but it was a cold of rebirth, cleansing and giving me energy again. I rolled and smoked two complete cigarettes before I heard heavy footsteps slamming up the stairs inside.

I went back in. The day deputy was named Kip Rolins. He was a balding blond man with a beard a Viking would have envied. He looked as if he could hold his own with just about any opponent you shoved at him.

He stuck his head in my hotel room door and said, "Stinks in here." Then: "Oh, God, I'm gonna get stuck telling his wife."

"Where's Nordberg?"

"He had to be in court this morning. He should be out any time now. But Missus Ralston's gonna find out about this before then. I better tell her before somebody else does."

I wondered if it made him feel official, telling a wife her husband was dead. A cynical thought but he didn't sound unhappy about it at all.

He reached inside the pocket of his knee-length winter coat and took out a nice tablet and a pencil. He had to take off his gloves to write.

"So how about telling me what happened here, Mr. Ford?"

I told him and I left.

Chapter 37

Just as I got to the street, I saw Loretta DeMeer going into the general store, a large straw basket hanging from her right arm. I thought of catching up to her but decided to visit the livery first.

A girl of maybe sixteen was raking out a stall when I got there.

"I guess I've never met you." I showed her my badge.

She stopped raking, leaned on the wooden handle. She had black pigtails hanging below the Western hat she wore. A snub nose and lively blue eyes made her cuter than I'd thought at first glance.

"I'm Judy Whalen. I suppose you're looking for Mr. Ralston."

"I'm sorry to say that Mr. Ralston's dead."

She didn't say anything, just gave me an odd stare, as if I'd just uttered the strangest words she'd ever heard.

"But he come over to the house last night and gave me the key and said I should open up for him the way I sometimes do. How come he's dead?"

"Because somebody murdered him."

"Oh, his poor wife. She's my aunt. You sure he's dead?" She was still struggling with the concept.

"I'm sure. But what I want to know is if you've seen him this morning?"

"No. He said he wouldn't be in till late in the afternoon."

"Anybody else come asking for him this morning?"

"No."

Then, without warning, tears formed in her eyes and began traveling down her cheeks. Silent crying. She seemed unaware of her tears. "Nobody had anything against Uncle Tim. Everybody liked him."

"Sure seemed that way."

"And gosh—my aunt was just in here."

"Where'd she go?"

"She said she was going to stop at the pharmacy."

"Thanks. I'll try to catch her."

"You know, everybody always said that my dad would go before Uncle Tim on account of his heart condition. But it turned out it was Uncle Tim who died before he did."

Still grappling with death. People spend their whole lives grappling with it.

Mrs. Ralston had been in the pharmacy but left; Mrs. Ralston had been in the dress shop but left. I caught up with her in the Catholic church, where the dress shop lady said she'd gone. The dress shop lady also told me that somebody had come into her shop and told her about Ralston dying. This person hadn't realized until too late that Mrs. Ralston was in the back of the store, listening. The dress shop lady had said that Mrs. Ralston had gone pretty crazy for a time. Completely inconsolable. The dress shop lady had poured three belts of whiskey down her, which had helped some; had at least, if nothing else, gotten her past her screaming. "I never heard anybody scream like Mrs. Ralston did right there at the first. It was scary to hear. Never heard anything like it."

She sat in the last pew, Mrs. Ralston did. The church was empty except for her. I sat next to her.

We didn't talk for a long time. She had a rosary and a small handkerchief in her hand. Her left hand trembled violently.

Finally, she said, "Some of this is your fault, Mr. Ford."

She sounded too calm. I was talking to a dead person.

"I suppose it is. I'm sorry, Mrs. Ralston."

"That'll be the worst thing of all, except for Tim dying."

"What will?"

"Hearing everybody say 'I'm sorry.' Over and over again."

"It's hard to know what else to say."

She wore a bulky cloth coat. She was child-small inside it. Her headscarf was black with small bright flowers celebrating spring. But right then in that ice-cold church, with a dead woman sitting next to me, spring seemed a long impossible way off.

"I need to ask you some questions, Mrs. Ralston."

"You don't care he's dead, do you?"

I hadn't realized until then that she hadn't looked at me yet. Not even a glance. She stared straight ahead at a wooden Christ on a wooden cross. This was a humble parish. No stained glass, no marble altar. The scent of incense hung melancholy on the air.

"I'm just doing my job, Mrs. Ralston."

"Your job." She finally looked at me. She was furious. "Your job is to go places and bring people misery. That's what your job is. My husband knew something but he was going to let it slide. But you wouldn't let him. You kept on him and on him. And you didn't care that if he told you what he knew, he'd be killed."

She was shouting by the end of it. Then, spent, she turned away to face the altar again.

After a time, I said, "Well, he didn't tell me anything, Mrs. Ralston, and he died anyway. Whoever killed him would have killed him, anyway."

"I'm sure it was Tremont. Tremont came sniffing around the same way you did."

Tremont.

"When was this?" I asked.

"Two times yesterday. Tim had to hide from Tremont just the way he had to hide from you."

"Did he ever tell you anything?"

"No."

Was she lying?

"Are you sure?"

"I'm sure. Now leave me alone. I never want to see you again. Ever. You understand? Not ever!"

Just then an old priest came in the side door at the back of the church. He needed a cane to walk. Her voice had been sharp. He said, "Is everything all right, Mrs. Ralston?"

"Yes, Father."

"I'm sorry about your husband, Mrs. Ralston."

"Thank you, Father."

She'd been right about one thing, anyway. She was going to hear a lot of sorrys in the next few days.

Chapter 38

Loretta DeMeer's wagon was still in front of the general store. There was one thing I needed answered and given what she'd said the other night, I was hoping she could answer it for me.

The general store smelled of pipe tobacco, saddle leather, coffee being heated on the stove, licorice, cottons—so many rich aromas. And so much promise. When you were young, a general store was like going to greed heaven. There were so many things you wanted to take home you couldn't quite cope with it. Of course you were limited to the few coins your dad had given you the night before so your money was no match for your greed.

I found her looking at pots and pans. I had no idea what the various shapes and sizes were used for. To me a pan was a pan.

"Well, there's a nice-looking man if I've ever seen one," she said. "Except you look a little tired."

"Too much going on. I need to get back East where things are calmer."

She was turning a pot back and forth and upside

down for inspection. "Now that's a new one. I've always heard about the Wild Wild East. We just rob banks and have range wars out here. We don't get into any of that decadence that goes on in big cities."

"I'll have to look into that when I get back there. I hadn't heard of it until you mentioned it."

I moved closer to her. She wore a brown corduroy coat lined with lamb's wool, a heavy sweater and dungarees. The sweater was pleasantly full with her breasts. I had the start of one of those totally unexpected and totally useless erections you get in public places.

But I'd moved closer with a purpose. I had to lower my voice. I surveyed the place. Nobody was close to us.

"You mentioned how much Mike Chaney got around. You mentioned a couple of married women he got pregnant."

She said, "You want to talk about that here?" Even though she whispered, she seemed uncomfortable. Her perfect composure was broken.

"All I need are the names."

Her gaze lifted and she said, "Why, Mr. Howard, how're you this morning?"

"Didn't see you come in, Mrs. DeMeer. I was in the back unpacking things and Ida didn't mention it. Just wanted to say hello."

My back was to him. I turned around and smiled at him. "Morning."

"I thought that was you, Mr. Ford. I was just going to ask if you people knew anything more about poor Ralston. He was in Rotary with me, you know."

He was a small, bald man who wore a leather

apron over a yellow shirt and a pair of work trousers. He had a yellow pencil stuck behind his ear.

"Sorry to say we don't, though I haven't checked in for a while."

"He sure was a good man."

"He sure was," Loretta DeMeer said. And I could tell she meant it. Her tone was rich with the troubled noise only death can put in a voice. She was thinking of Ralston's mortality but she was also thinking of her own. I was doing the same thing.

"Well, there'll be a lot of people at the funeral, that's for sure," Mr. Howard said. "He was very well liked in this town." He nodded to Loretta and then to me. "Well, sorry to interrupt your conversation, folks. Time for me to get back to work."

"Seems like a decent man," I said after he'd left.

"You've got the wrong impression of this town, Noah. Most of the people here are decent. You've just run into a lot of murders. And that's not typical, believe me."

I lowered my voice again. "I need to know the names of the two women you were going to tell me about."

And then she told me. One of the women had moved away with her husband two years before, the husband apparently assuming the child was his. But then she told me the name of the other woman. The one still there. And when she told me I said to myself no, not possible. But then possible—maybe more than possible.

She said something else but I didn't hear.

Then: "What's wrong, Noah?"

"I need to get to the doc's office."

"Aren't you feeling well?"

"I'm feeling fine—just a little stupid is all."

I arrived in time to see Wendy Nordberg leaving the doc's office. She made a pretty mother, her child held so tenderly.

She must have heard me coming because she looked up suddenly. And just as suddenly turned away from the shoveled walk leading to the main street. She abruptly took a path that led down along the river. I wondered if she knew why I was looking for her. That didn't make any sense. How could she know?

I walked faster. But so did she. She was walking along a shoveled path next to the river. It was probably a five-foot drop to the ice- and snow-covered water.

"Mrs. Nordberg! Wait for me! I need to talk to you!"

I moved as fast as I could along the path, too fast, because I lost my footing and slammed into an oak tree next to the path.

I was knocked unconscious. Not for more than a few seconds. But for those seconds there was—nothing. Not even pain. But the pain was there waiting for me when I returned to the world.

I had a headache that no hangover could ever equal. Somebody had sawed right through my skull, right down the middle. I touched fingers to the top of my forehead and felt hot blood there. I moved my fingers gently around the trail of blood and then I came to the wound. It wasn't big, it wasn't deep. But it had been sufficient to knock me out.

Then I remembered Mrs. Nordberg.

I grabbed on to the tree that had nearly done me in and pulled myself to my feet. I had to blink my eyes several times to clear my vision. I decided against shaking my head. It might roll off.

I saw her way down the river trail. She was still moving pretty fast but not as fast as she had been. Carrying a baby had to take its toll on strength and energy, especially when you were trying not to slip and fall.

I started out running down the slope to the trail but that didn't last long. My head couldn't take the punishment of speed. I slowed down to a fast, awkward walk. I was afraid of tumbling again. For at that point I might not recover as fast as I had before. At that point—there was at least the possibility—I might not recover at all. People died in all sorts of winter-related accidents.

I gained on her steadily. She looked back once and saw me.

The only warm part of me was the trickle of blood on my forehead. I really did need to get that stitched up.

I had almost caught up to her. "I just want to talk to you, Mrs. Nordberg! Let's just stop and talk!"

I made my voice as cordial as I could.

But she didn't turn around again. She increased her speed by doubling the number of mincing little steps she took. She wanted to hurry but she wanted to be safe, too.

I was almost able to reach out and grab her shoulder when it happened. The accident had the air of unreality about it—the mind's first impulse to reject it as impossible—but that didn't stop it from being real indeed.

In other circumstances, a stage comedy for instance, what happened might even have been humorous.

You have this woman hurrying along a path adjacent to the river five feet below. Clutching her baby as if her—their—lives depended on it. That noblest of all creatures—the mother protecting her child.

And then it happened.

She stumbled or started sliding. Whichever it was, she lost her grip on the infant she was carrying. And the baby, still swaddled in baby blankets, popped from her arms. It took to the air. And I think she and I both became paralyzed at the same instant, watching the arc of the child as it flew upward into the air. It seemed to hover there for a very long time—the way certain terrible moments in nightmares seem to linger—and it then began a descent to the icy river, where moments later it crashed.

She found her voice. Her scream was so piercing, so helpless, so horrified that I doubted I would ever be able to get it out of my mind.

Then I found my legs. Instinct took over then. I stepped to the edge of the trail.

Mrs. Nordberg was still screaming, crying out for her child. No sound sadder than that.

In that instant, I calculated that the ice would be strong enough to hold me when I slammed onto its surface. If it wasn't, there was a good chance I'd smash through it and drown in the icy waters below. There wasn't the faintest hope that Mrs. Nordberg would be able to save me. Or even lend a hand in that effort. She wanted her daughter. That was her only concern. And I couldn't blame her.

I jumped.

As I landed, my full weight touching the ice for the first time, I heard a muted cracking sound. Would it hold me? I could see the infant sitting maybe ten yards from me. When it landed, it had skidded up river. Making things even more difficult.

Mrs. Nordberg teetered on the edge of the snow above the river. She was steeling herself for a jump to the ice.

I shouted, "Let me get her, Mrs. Nordberg!"

But I doubted she could hear me. Her only reality was the baby on the ice below her. Her baby.

I started moving toward it. The deep cracking sound came again. My face was sheathed with sweat that made me tremble. The icy water would take care of the sweat. Unless I was very lucky, it would take care of me, too.

I started carefully, slowly across the ten yards separating me from the infant.

At that moment, Mrs. Nordberg decided to jump. The effect was startling. She seemed to hang in the air, irrespective of time and gravity, just as her infant had after popping from her mom's arms.

This time the cracking sound was much more pronounced. She was a thin body but heavy enough to make a difference on that section of ice. She landed on her hands and knees. A thin line, thin as a thread, appeared in the ice between me and the baby. The woman was in no condition—she was still on her hands and knees—to grab her baby in case the crack got wider and a hole opened up in the ice.

I moved as fast as I could toward the kid. Saving her was the only thought in my mind. Nothing else mattered.

I covered five feet of ice, six, seven. And then the infant was within my reach. I bent down and picked up the blankets that hid the infant.

The big thing was to make sure that the infant had survived the fall. Sometimes they survived catastrophes; sometimes minor injuries killed them.

I guess in my frenzy, wanting to get the blankets off her so that I could see her face and make sure she was all right—I guess in that second I didn't notice how little the blankets weighed.

But then I began undoing the blankets that kept her warm and hid her from public view.

There was no baby inside.

I was holding only a bundle of small bunched blankets that had been safety-pinned together to resemble the shape of a baby.

Chapter 39

"Nordberg wasn't home when I got there," Doc Tomkins said, "but Wendy was. She was sitting in this rocking chair with the baby in her lap, rocking back and forth. I don't think I've ever seen anybody who looked like that. Her eyes, I mean. They were totally—vacant. I don't know any other way to describe them. This beautiful little house and you look in the window and there's nothing inside. No people, no furniture, nothing.

"I'd come out there because Sheriff Nordberg had stopped by and said that the baby was pretty sick. That was the first time I realized that that's what he always called her. 'The baby.' Not 'his' baby or 'her baby' or even 'their baby.' He didn't look worried or sad or anything that night. If anything, he looked angry. I thought maybe that was the way he reacted to a sick baby. That's how some people react to any sort of medical problem. They get mad.

"Well, Wendy was a favorite of mine. And so was her little girl. They were just such sweet, quiet little people. Never knew a baby who made as little fuss.

So I went out there right away and I see her in this rocking chair and I see the baby in her lap and I see that she's got the baby all covered up. I spoke to Wendy a couple of times. But her expression didn't change. She just sat in the chair and rocked back and forth. And stared. I wondered what she was seeing. In her mind, I mean. Something had obviously happened that she couldn't face up to.

"So I leaned over and turned the cover back and there was the baby and I knew right away she was dead. I remembered how sharp my breath was in the house when I realized that she was sitting there rocking a dead baby.

"But Wendy was so far gone, she didn't even seem to know what I was doing when I took the baby from her. I carried her over to their table and turned up the lamp and examined her right there.

"Didn't take a genius to figure out what had happened. The left side of the baby's head was stove in. The wound was deep and raw, I could see bone there under the blood. Then I happened to notice some kind of smear on the wall behind where Wendy sat in the rocking chair.

"I picked up the lamp and went over there and got a close look. You could see where somebody had smashed her head against the wall. There was blood and hair and flecks of bone in this smear I was looking at. And I didn't have to think real hard about who'd done it. It sure hadn't been Wendy. Not the way she loved that little girl.

"I wrapped the baby up and went looking for some whiskey. Wendy didn't want any of it at first but I made her take it. And it was funny, after about three belts—and she hadn't said a single word the whole time—she just sat there staring straight ahead and started shuddering. Never saw a person thrash around that way. She was like some contraption that was going to fly apart in bits and pieces.

"I right away dug in my bag and got her a sedative and I gave it to her. I sat right next to her on a footstool, holding her hand until the shuddering stopped when the sedative took hold of her.

"And that was when she told me everything. How Nordberg would beat her from their wedding night on. That he always called her a whore, even though she'd really been a virgin at that time. Not even Mike Chaney had slept with her at that point, though she'd gone out with him for three years before Nordberg even came to town. She wanted a baby. That was all she thought about. Having a baby. She'd never been a real social girl so she figured she'd finally get a true friend who she could take care of. A baby.

"But Nordberg wouldn't touch her after the first six months of their marriage. He'd go into these rages and accuse her of giving him some kind of disease. She knew he was sneaking off and seeing girls at the bawdyhouse. But his own wife he wouldn't have anything to do with.

"Then he started raping her. That's what she called it. He'd come home drunk and throw her against the wall and rape her. And then he'd beat her afterward.

"She told her folks this but they're religious people and they told her that the Bible said a woman should answer only to her husband, not carry tales of him to others. A man needed his dignity and she was giving him a bad name. Besides, these things always worked out. That was the sign of a good marriage. Having things work out.

"Then one night when he was gone, she went out for a walk as she did a lot on spring nights. And ran into Mike Chaney. That's how he explained it, anyway. Completely coincidental. He just happened to be walking down the same grassy lane she was. She had the sense that he'd followed her but she didn't really care.

"That night she slept with him. She still had feelings for him. Not love, she told me. She'd grown up enough to see that he was a showboat as much as anything. That he wasn't robbing Flannery's banks to help people around here—he was doing it to humiliate Flannery and to make a name for himself.

"She got pregnant. There was no doubt it was Mike's child. When Nordberg accused her of sleeping with somebody else, she told him that he wasn't remembering the night when he'd thrown her on the bed and taken her from behind. She told him he'd never been up that far inside of her before, that's how she'd gotten pregnant. She said he believed her for a while.

"But he couldn't let go of the notion that Mike was the baby's father. He got to the point where he didn't want to even look at the child, let alone hold it or even touch it.

"And then one night he came home drunk and wild and took the baby by her ankles and smashed her head against the wall. That was when I got involved in it all. And I'm not proud I didn't speak up. I'm too old to move anywhere else. And I didn't have

•

any proof that Nordberg did it. It could have been Wendy herself, though I knew better.

"Nordberg wasn't anybody I could go up against. He has too many friends in this town. I rode out there the next morning to see how Wendy was. She came to the door holding those blankets all wrapped up and pretending her baby was inside. Her baby dying and all—she lost her mind. She sat in the rocking chair with all those blankets bundled together and talked about her baby as if she was still alive. I think Nordberg buried the real baby somewhere and the fact that Wendy was carrying those bundled-up blankets all over town was fine with him. People thought the real baby was still alive.

"I imagine with what happened this morning—the way you described her on the ice—I imagine she's even worse off mentally than she was before. You brought her over here but while we were in here talking, Ford, she left. The Lord alone knows where's she gone now."

Chapter 40

The ride out to Nordberg's place was cold. The wind was up, doing its best to ruin the sunny day. I was still trying to sort it all out. It was beginning to come clear. Nordberg didn't just want Mike Chaney dead, he wanted him discredited. The town thought Mike Chaney was a hero until he started killing people. Or until Nordberg made it look as if Chaney was killing people. But it was Nordberg who'd killed them all.

His only problem was when he rode out and killed Chaney and Pepper and Connelly. He set it up to make it look as if Flannery had murdered them. And who wouldn't believe it? Everybody knew how much Flannery hated Chaney. And he'd have to kill the agents with Chaney because they might be able to identify him.

On the way out to Nordberg's that morning, I'd stopped by Mrs. Ralston's place. She finally admitted that her husband had told her it was Nordberg who'd taken his horse from the livery the afternoon Chaney and the others had died. And the maid at

Flannery's mansion confirmed to me that Nordberg was one of the men who'd been given the command words to calm the Dobermans. Flannery and Nordberg had done a lot of hunting together. Flannery had shown off his dogs many times to Nordberg and trusted Nordberg to know the secret words. With the dogs subdued, it had been easy for Nordberg to sneak into the mansion and set up Flannery's fake suicide. And then by insisting to me that it *had* been faked, he threw suspicion off himself.

Smoke from the tin chimney. A pair of jittery squirrels raising their heads as I approached the Nordberg place. Raising their heads and then scampering away. A hefty gray tomcat sat in the window, watching me with great interest.

There was no good place to hide at the front of the house. All I could do was grab my carbine and circle wide to the rear of the place.

Nordberg's horse was there. The saddlebags bulged. The horse was ready to go.

There was a single window in back and that was where he fired from. The shot got me in the left shoulder with such force that it spun me half around. It also saved my life by knocking me to the ground, in time to elude the other two shots that rang out afterward.

Shock. Pain. Confusion. Pain. I knew that he'd be out the back door to finish me. I buried my face in the snow, keeping it there until my cheeks felt frozen hard. I had to stay clearheaded. The snow stunned me into full consciousness, enough so that I was able to crawl over to a pile of firewood and drag myself behind it.

I wondered why he hadn't come after me already. He would certainly be eager to kill me. I was a loose end he needed to tie up before he escaped town and went somewhere to start a new life for himself. As much as the Old West was quickly becoming the New West, there were still many places a man could hide and start a new life somewhere. There was always the chance that somebody would appear from your past and recognize you. But a man like Nordberg, running away and starting fresh was the only chance he had.

A scream, a gunshot, a fainter scream.

Wendy. He'd shot and probably killed Wendy. That shouldn't have surprised me—it was his hatred of her that had driven him to kill all those people—but still, lying there in the snow, the smell of damp wood filling my nostrils on that fine bright blue-skyed winter day, the screams and the single shot seemed more violent than anything I'd yet encountered in that town. Crazy Wendy, carrying those blankets around and convinced her real child was inside them. Crazy Nordberg, so given to rage and hatred, but able to conceal it in a character he'd created for himself—the quiet, sensible, dutiful town sheriff, a man respected by just about everybody in the community. Not seeming to understand—or maybe not caring to understand—that one killing necessitated another and then another and then another.

Until that moment.

The scream and the gunshot and the second, weaker scream.

The bleeding was getting bad by then. I sopped up as much of the blood as I could with my coat. But soon enough the whole side of the coat would be soaked.

Not a sound from inside. A windswept silence. That deep solemn song of wind fanning the pines in back of Nordberg's property. Then a sound I didn't recognize at first. My own sound, a low deep moan. Me.

The back door opening. Footsteps on the stoop. Nordberg.

He didn't say anything. He just put two bullets into the three-foot-high pile of firewood I was hiding behind. It was the only place I could possibly be. He knew he'd wounded me, that I probably wasn't in any condition to make it back to the pines. Therefore I was behind the firewood.

"You knew whose baby that was all along, didn't you, Ford? I bet a lot of people did. And I bet they got a lot of good laughs out of it, too. Poor stupid Nordberg. Too dumb to know that Mike Chaney was fucking his wife all the time after Nordberg married her. Well, I took care of that slut. And now I'm gonna finish it up with you."

Footsteps on the stoop. Then crunching into the snow.

There was a bad problem by then. I was starting to black out every thirty seconds or so. Not for long. But long enough so that I might not be able to defend myself. Even if he killed me, I wanted to put a couple of bullets into him. Maybe I couldn't take him with me but I sure wanted him to remember me.

I eased myself up on my haunches. My breath came in raw gasps. As soon as he got near, I was going to jerk myself up and start firing. It was better than just letting him shoot me.

He put two more bullets into the firewood. A small piece of wood flew into my left eye, momentarily blinding it. My left arm was useless because of the wound. And my right hand was needed to hold my gun. I had to live with the blinking left eye.

He didn't try to walk soft. He sounded like he was purposely walking heavy. Trying to unnerve me.

Closer and closer and closer.

I gripped my .44 hard. Got ready to lurch up as far as I could and fire two, three times. Uselessly, probably. But right then I didn't give a damn. I just felt this animal anger.

Closer and closer and—

I stood up. Or tried to. I even got a couple of shots off. But the trouble was that even as I was standing up my legs were shaking so badly from the blood loss and shock of the wound—even as I was standing I was falling over backward.

He came around the firewood and looked down at me on my back. In the fall, my gun had slipped from my hand and was lost in the snow.

"Maybe you fucked her, too. I never thought of that till just right now, Ford. You probably fucked her, too, didn't you?"

He was gone. Way gone. He'd loved her and hated her. And finally he'd killed her. But he still wasn't sated. He was pure hate crazy by then. Imagining that I'd slept with her. Pure hate crazy.

He raised his .45.

For me there was just pain and nuisance. My shoulder pounded with pain. And my left eye kept blinking and watering over.

I'd always thought about how I would die. I'd seen brave men shit their pants and beg to live. But I couldn't do that because all I was going to have out there on that nowhere patch of windswept land was a bit of dignity. And dignity wouldn't matter to him or the unknown place I was headed for. But it mattered to me because it was the only comfort I had.

"Go on and kill me, you crazy fucker. Just get it over with."

He was about to oblige me when the left side of his head blew up, firing a heft of bloody hair up against the blue sky. He lived just long enough to look surprised. And then he fell face forward, his gun firing off a last round into the snow.

And then there was just the wind and my throbbing shoulder.

And after a time, the sobbing.

It took me a long time to get up. And I fell down twice before I reached her.

Seeing my wound and my condition seemed to slap Wendy back to reality. She still had the carbine she'd used to kill him. She sat on the stoop. She seemed unaware of how bloody her dress was. He'd gotten her in the chest.

She looked so pretty and aggrieved and insane sitting there in her blood-soaked gingham, that sweet little face that would never know a smile again. And maybe that wouldn't matter to her anyway because someday she would have to admit to herself that her child was dead.

Or so I thought.

I took two lumbering steps toward her just as she leaned over backward, sprawling over the stoop. Dead.

Chapter 41

I stayed a few days longer than I'd planned. Jen and Clarice were there every day. Clarice would soon become her adopted daughter.

Jen also decided that the two-bed hospital was no place for a federal man to recover his strength. I figured she had her hands full with Clarice, but she took me to her place, the scandal of it be damned, and for four days running we played nurse and patient. She was a most generous nurse, giving all of her body and at least some of her soul to making me feel better.

I never wanted to get better but dammit I did. On a frosty Sunday morning, she kissed me goodbye on the depot platform. She went back to live down the scandal and I went on to Washington to find out who I was supposed to kill next.